Black
Pansies

Smoke Rising, Sorrow, and the Deep
Yearning for Everlasting Love.

Marlene F. Cheng

Copyright reference number   © 663257740013435960   2022-04-01

Cover Design is by Mary Orr.

Cover photograph is a paid copy from Shutterstock.

Author's photo is by Leona Lilith.

ISBN.

Soft cover.

eBook.

Dedication

This book is dedicated to the several displaced men, women, and children of the world.

May you find a place of graced belonging.

To the bouquet of memories that I have of my father, Jack Gladdish, who provided sheltered belonging for us all, in the wildness of the Canadian Prairies and, later, in the Selkirk and Monashee mountains of British Columbia, where we might inhabit deeper dreams.

Table of Contents

Backstory book

Have you read *The Madam's Friend*? It's the fourth book in the Love is Forever series and is great backstory for *Black Pansies*.

Check it out on my website: marlenecheng.com or pick it up at Amazon.com or Amazon.ca

Are you enjoying *Black Pansies*?
Please consider leaving a short review or a few positive words on any of the following sites:

amazon.com/author/marlenecheng
goodreads.com/marlenecheng
marlenecheng.com

I would love to hear from you at marlene.cheng@telus.net. I read all comments
and respond.
THANK YOU

What Beta Readers
are saying about Black Pansies.

"Black Pansies is all about love. Love of the self, family, and that one special person to share your life with. It was a truly beautiful experience to read Fiza's journey as she understood her identity and navigated towards her future."
—Worthy Writers Editing

"Terrible loss and devastating heartbreak, passionate love and immense joy fill the pages of Black Pansies. It is fiercely inspiring and deeply emotional."
—A Beta Reader, Great Britain

"A sweeping tale that transports readers between war-torn South Sudan and Ornskoldsvik, Sweden where Fiza, an adoptee, and David, a war veteran, struggle with heartbreaking pasts. They fight ferociously, to find a path forward to everlasting love, together. Black Pansies is compelling in every aspect. Be prepared for tears of excruciating sadness and of great joy." **— M.L. A Beta Reader, British Columbia, Canada**

"A Compelling, heart-rending story about love and loss, pain and prejudice, and the roots that bind families. Highly recommended."
—A Beta Reader, Canada

Praise For
Marlene's Other Books.

"Though the plot kept me turning pages eager to see what was going to happen next, I was drawn to the relationship of the Madame and her friend - I was intrigued with what connected them and how those bonds thrived. Honestly, I was drawn into the web of all the relationships in this wonderful story!"

—Diana Germain, Beta Reader, Canada

"One of the best new voices in fiction today."

—Midwest BookReview

"Warm, psychologically introspective, culturally, and spiritually revealing, and filled with the gentle flow of interconnected lives, *A Mystical Embrace* enhances the bond series by pursing the threads of previous books."

—Diane Donovan, Author/Editor,
California Bookwatch

"*A Mystical Embrace* is a fantastic journey that takes readers to the innermost corners of the human heart."

—Readers' Favorite

"I let the depth of the story and the memorable characters fill my thoughts introspectively. The tragedy and loss brought into focus that which is most important to us all, and I am grateful. It helped me to live more in the present."

—Dr. Kim, DDM, Maple Ridge, BC

"Marlene writes with great facility. Her writing is intelligent: her prose is poetic."

—Dr. David Leung, MBBS, FRCPC,
certified psychiatrist

Introduction

Black Pansies: Smoke Rising, Sorrow, and the Deep Yearning for Everlasting Love is a spinoff from the *Love is Forever* series.

Fiza (see the family tree) was adopted by Doctors Tijay and Z. They brought her from South Sudan to Ornskoldsvik, Sweden when she was in her early teens. She appreciated the gifts that her new country offered: family, friendship, home, education, opportunities. Her powerful survival skills helped her to succeed. But she is haunted by her past.

Fiza narrates this book, which begins when she is an adult, living independently in a turret in Ornskoldsvik and overseeing the family enterprise—The Store.

The Family Tree

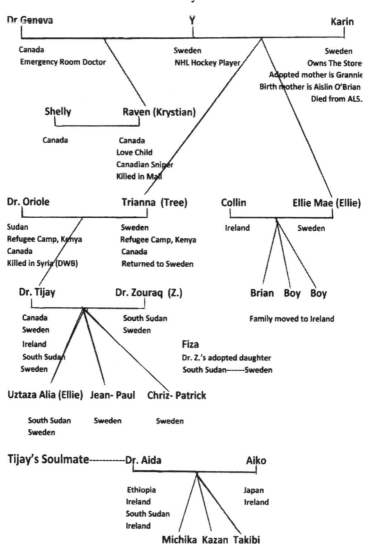

Dr Geneva — **Y** — **Karin**

Canada
Emergency Room Doctor

Sweden
NHL Hockey Player

Sweden
Owns The Store
Adopted mother is Grannie
Birth mother is Aislin O'Brian
Died from ALS.

Shelly — **Raven (Krystian)**

Canada

Canada
Love Child
Canadian Sniper
Killed in Mali

Dr. Oriole — **Trianna (Tree)** — **Collin** — **Ellie Mae (Ellie)**

Sudan
Refugee Camp, Kenya
Canada
Killed in Syria (DWB)

Sweden
Refugee Camp, Kenya
Canada
Returned to Sweden

Ireland

Sweden

Dr. Tijay — **Dr. Zouraq (Z.)**

Brian   Boy   Boy

Canada
Sweden
Ireland
South Sudan
Sweden

South Sudan
Sweden

Fiza
Dr. Z.'s adopted daughter
South Sudan-------Sweden

Family moved to Ireland

Uztaza Alia (Ellie)   Jean- Paul   Chriz- Patrick

South Sudan
Sweden

Sweden

Sweden

Tijay's Soulmate----------**Dr. Aida** — **Aiko**

Ethiopia
Ireland
South Sudan
Ireland

Japan
Ireland

Michika Kazan Takibi

Part One
Ornskoldsvik, Sweden

Scene One
The Loom

I felt a presence. A hint of prickliness. A dash of daring. Although I was determined to finish adding the invoices to the Excel chart, the full dollop of this force, demanding my attention, melted my resolve. I looked up.

There he was. A handsome specimen with a smirk, leaning against the door frame.

I gasped. My heart quickened. My tongue tied in knots, leaving no room for words. My hands became all thumbs as I tried to close the laptop and roll myself back from the desk. I leapt up, wrapping my arms around myself, trying to keep my heart from escaping from my chest. No man had ever unbalanced me like this.

"Y-yes," I said. "How can I help you?"

"There was a SUE nameplate at the front desk, but there wasn't a Sue in sight. I hung my coat on the stand and decided to wander. Your door was open... You look flustered," he added, while his dark eyes wandered down my V-neck shirt. "Are you the one who advertised for a man's help?" He ran his fingers through his slightly grown out haircut, smoothed down his in-fashion shadow-beard, then brandished a piece of paper. I recognized the ad I had pinned on the Starbucks' board, asking for help to assemble a loom. I felt a flush rising between my breasts. "You look pretty in pink," he said, probably noticing.

"Y-yes. Have you come to apply for the job?" I asked, raising an eyebrow.

"That's why I'm here."

"W-well then. You can fill out the form at the front desk."

"There's no Sue," he reminded me. "I'm David. And you?"

"Fiza," I answered, and offered my hand.

He shook it. "Pleased to meet you. What an interesting name."

His hand was warm. His grip firm, reassuring. When he removed it, I thought, *there's something more to this man than what he's trying to portray. Why did I, in that moment, not want him to let me go?*

"It was the name, on your ad, that piqued my curiosity—Fiza—and it suits its owner to a T. But I'm curious about the loom. I've come to assemble it."

How cocky, I thought. *Remind him to fill out the application form. Dismiss him. When he's gone, tear up the form.*

He might have read my thoughts, but they didn't deter him.

"Well then, are you going to show me the loom?" he asked.

Ooof, I thought. *What the heck? The ad has been up three weeks and no one else has showed up. No harm in letting him have a look.* "Yes, of course. She's housed behind The Store. We had the room built-on just for Gertrude. I'll show you. You'll need your coat," I said, taking mine from its hanger. "It's a short walk outside. I stepped past him. "This way, please."

"Gertrude?" he queried in an eye-rolling manner. We walked to Gertrude's Place, the name I had given to the loom's home.

I opened the door, and we stepped in. "Poof! It's hot in here." He peeled off his coat.

"We've had an exceptionally cold February, as you probably know, and the staff jack up the thermostat in here. We don't want the loom parts to freeze." *Should I leave my coat on? Let the perspiration bead on my brow and run black rivulets through my whitening makeup?* "You can hang your coat here." I put mine on a hook.

"Turn down the furnace. I'll leave the door ajar. This place needs airing out," he said.

"As you can see, I had the crates lined up by number. The person who took the loom apart did it methodically. The number one crate has the first parts that were disassembled," I explained. "I've taken off the lids to have a look."

With a disgruntled stare, he investigated the crates. "All I can see, and smell, is antique metal and rotting wood," he said. "Why don't you scrap all these junk parts and buy something new that I could help you assemble? Ikea probably sells these."

I was bruised. I was going to explain how precious this bespoke antique Dobcross shuttle loom was, but he had called her junk. *I've changed my mind. You arrogant, insensitive jerk.*

"Then, Mr. David, we should call it a day. Give me time to think about what you have said. Leave your card at the front desk. Sue will contact you when, or if, I need your service." Sue had been with our family-run enterprise, which we called The Store, for as long as I can remember. She would know how to handle Mr. David. "And by the way," I added, "the name Fiza represents deeply who I am. I am from the proud people of South Sudan." *There,* I thought, *I've had the last word. I'm proud of myself.* Being black and trying to fit in the white world of Ornskoldsvik, Sweden, I most often am reticent. *I stood my ground. Good on you, girl.*

"Did it come with any how-to papers?" he asked. It was as if he hadn't heard a word of what I said.

Now what should I do? Ooof. What the heck. I handed him a thick folder, and said, "The person who disassembled her recorded measurements of the parts and took lots of pictures."

"I'll have a look-see what the devil we have here," he said. He knelt on the floor and spread out the photos in the order that the loom should be reassembled, becoming engrossed. He completely ignored me. I didn't want to disturb him, so I kept my mouth shut, but my mind wasn't. Thoughts and questions about this strange stranger twirled in there like gale force winds.

To quell the turmoil, I shifted my thoughts to Gertrude and how she had come to be mine.

My grandmother's sister, my Grand Aunt Ellie, married an Irishman and moved to Ireland long before I came to Sweden. One day she was out roaming the Connemara hills, checking on their flocks of sheep, enjoying the fresh air that swept up from the sea. She came upon an abandoned, run-down building. No one had ever spoken of it. She was curious and decided to check it out. Through an opening she saw that the roof had collapsed onto this enormous machine. Farming equipment, she assumed. When she got home, she told her husband about her adventure and what she had found.

Grand Aunt Ellie and Uncle Collin went to investigate. What they discovered was most surprising. It wasn't farming equipment, after all. It was Gertrude.

When Grand Aunt Ellie left Ornskoldsvik for Ireland, she had to abandon the family enterprise—The Store—that she had invested her heart and soul in. As soon as she saw Gertrude, she knew she belonged in The Store, and because I was the overseer, she gave her to me. She had Gertrude carefully taken apart, crated, and shipped.

When he looked up and asked, "Do you have a measuring tape?" I jerked in surprise. I thought he had forgotten that I was waiting. When I handed the tape to him, he stood up, surveying the room. "Where do you want this monster to sit?"

"I want room to be able to walk around her," I said, "but I don't want her taking up the center of the space. I'm hoping there'll be room for supply shelves and we mustn't forget to factor in the space for the warper."

"We'll start three feet back from the door wall," he decided. "Can you get some chalk and string from The Store? I need to recheck some calculations."

We drew chalk lines on the floor outlining the space the loom would take. He studied it, consulting the photos. Unsatisfied, he erased the chalk lines by kicking them with his expensive-looking loafers. "We'll move it two feet that way and six inches back towards the wall," he said. "Hold the tape."

After the third try to get the loom situated just how he wanted it, my back was killing me, and the chalk dust had me sneezing. I raised one eyebrow and uttered, "Ooof." This Ooof was a mixture of exasperation and a tinge of hope.

David stretched. "Do you think I could bring my dog from the car? He'll need a drink."

"That will be fine," I said. *Why would anyone bring his dog to a job interview?* "I need a break. Would you like a beer? Or—"

"I need a coffee. Is that possible?"

"Of course, and how—?"

"Black."

"Gotcha."

"I won't be long."

I went to the kitchen, put on the coffee pot, then took a couple of apple scones from the well-stocked pantry to warm in the toaster oven. When we had this space built, I had a bathroom and a kitchen put in, so whoever was working here didn't have to run back and forth to The Store, especially if the weather was inclement.

I sat on my favorite chair and looked out to the trees beyond the kitchen window.

Why was he being so gruff? So blunt? I guessed from his accent that he was probably from the U.S. What was he doing here in Sweden? I wondered if his rough exterior was a show. Perhaps, he didn't want me to see a *softie*.

Why was I letting this man cow me? Probably because I was losing hope, thinking that Gertrude was doomed to be a rusty pile of broken dreams. I didn't want to let Grand Auntie down. I knew she had dreams of glory for the loom. David, even with his attitude, might be my only chance.

Besides, I was intuiting that a nice person was somewhere under all the gruff. Or maybe it was wishful thinking. I would let time tell whether I should kick him out.

Scene Two

Meeting Prince, the Dog

Prince, as I learned to call him, was huge, like a shiny-coated, well-groomed pony. He was all movement, pouncing excitedly on his owner. I never had a pet. Dogs of my childhood were wild. They were survival scavengers, usually considered rabid.

With all Prince's leaping, I thought he might attack. He frightened me. "Oh my," was my first reaction and my hands went to my mouth.

David said, "He senses that you are nervous. Don't be afraid." He reached for my hand and urged me to come close. "He's a gentle giant. There's no need to be afraid."

Tentatively I touched the dog, then progressively, I was able to stroke the top of his head. David gave him a command and he lay down. I kneeled and continued to stroke him. Prince licked my hand. "He likes you," David said and put a treat from his pocket in my flattened hand. When David said okay, Prince gently took the treat. "Pat him and tell him he's a good boy," David continued. "Bed," he commanded Prince. "Come," he commanded me. "Let me show you something. These long crates are the end frames. I want to stand them in place first. They are too heavy for you and me to move. Round up a couple of strong men and phone me at this number to arrange a time." He handed me a card. "What about that coffee?"

"Come to the kitchen." *You're catching on*, I thought. *Great command.*

He sat at the small table, stretched out his legs, and drank half his coffee in one gulp. "Prince is a mixture. Part Mastiff but mostly German Shepherd. He's intelligent and learns commands easily. I don't think he does it for the treats, but to please me. When I say good boy and ruffle his fur, he senses my happiness. But he has a mind of his own. If he doesn't feel like performing, he closes his eyes and ignores me," he commented.

"Have you had him long?" I asked.

"He's two years old. I've had him since he was a puppy. What a strange looking creature he was—huge head and paws. I'll tell you how I got him, but that's a story for another day." He picked up what was left of his scone and said, "I'll be leaving now. Prince and I need to go for a run at the beach." He gathered Prince's things, while finishing his scone, then said, "Phone when you've organized help." Without another word, they were gone.

Wow! What a day. What kind of adventure just blew through this place? I looked at David's card. It was from an engineering firm. *Mechanical? They like taking things apart, seeing how they work. Perhaps I've lucked out after all.*

Scene Three
Authenticity

David and Prince came sporadically. I wanted a commitment. I needed to know what days he would be working, so I asked, "How can I schedule your working days?"

"I have a day job and will come most weekends and some evenings if time allows."

"Oh. Can't you be more specific?"

"My day job is demanding. I've taken on your loom as a hobby. It relaxes me. Your ad said 'help wanted to assemble a loom.' It didn't specify that I had to tie myself down to a scheduled commitment. I'm enjoying working on the loom, but if you need someone to come more consistently, put up another ad at Starbucks."

"At your pace, how long do you think the job will take?" I asked, trying to get a handle on the situation. I had never dealt with an employee who didn't fit into company rules. When I had asked him earlier to give his information to the secretary, he scoffed.

"Sue controls payroll. If you don't give your particulars, you won't get paid." I had said, firmly.

"Was I asking to be paid?"

"Every employee gets paid," I explained.

"Then, I guess I'm not an employee. Do you want me to work on the loom? Yes, or no?"

I was over-the-top excited that we were getting started with Gertrude. A couple husbands of the ladies from The Store helped David get the end frames upright and in position. Under David's supervision, they moved crates closer to where their parts would fit. I was unaware how much work there had to be done to get Gertrude working, but I was enthusiastic and impatient and had answered yes. I would think of some other way to pay him for his work, perhaps a holiday in the sun.

His answer to how long it might take was evasive. "How high is the moon?" he asked. "And do you think man will ever live there?"

How frustrating. Maybe that's the price I must pay to see my dream come true. My goal is to weave heirloom blankets on this antique loom. If I want the process to be enjoyable, then I must stop fretting. Besides, I can't devote full time to it. I still have my job at The Store. Sue's been complaining that they are missing their overseer. *What's my hurry, anyway?*

We took coffee breaks and had interesting conversations. It seemed to amuse him that I cuddled my coffee mug with both hands. "Why do you do that?" he asked.

"I'm enjoying the full experience," I answered.

"I did something today I hope will help you enjoy the full experience of your Gertrude," he said. "I wanted to surprise you."

"Oh? And what is that?"

"Let's take our coffee to the loom. I'll show you."

On our walk, I thought, *am I seeing that softie part that he tries so hard to hide?*

"Stand there," he pointed.

He stood on a short ladder he had leaned against the end frame that faced the front and took away a cloth he had hung on it. "Can you read it? I cleaned and polished it."

"Yes, I can." There was a stamp: Hutchinson, Hollingworth and Company 1910 Dobcross. "Oh, how wonderful. That means she really is authentic. That company always put that stamp on their looms. Thank you, David, for the lovely surprise. Come down. Let's lift our coffee cups to her."

"Skal, Gertrude," I said.

"Do you mind if I call her Gertie?" he asked. "I'm beginning to think of her as a friend."

"As you please," I said.

"Skal, Gertie. Here's to your future."

We clinked our coffee cups.

Scene Four
On The Beach

I couldn't remember a spring day being so warm.

We were working on the last crate. Each part, as it was removed, had to be examined and labeled. I entered it in an inventory book, leaving a space for a photo. "Make a note," David said. "The wood, where I've marked on that part, needs to be replaced."

Sue came. "My gosh," she commented, "it smells like one hundred-year-old grease in here. The air is repressive. I'll have some fans brought over. Heat was expected, but I wasn't prepared for the stink. Would you like some cold drinks from the kitchen?"

"You're an angel," David answered. "I brought some iced tea. It is thick with orange and lemon peels and has a handful of mint and basil leaves. You must be careful pouring it. All that stuff could go plop in the glass, making a mess. It's in the fridge."

When she came back, she pulled up a chair. David and I sat on the floor. "Well?" she asked. "How's it going?"

"It may not look like much," David said, "but we've accomplished lots. When we finish this last crate, we'll know which parts need to be ordered."

"I'll have to research to find out where to get them," I said.

"Heaven only knows how long it'll take for them to come," David added. "But we'll stick to a methodical plan, not jumping ahead. If a part hasn't arrived, we'll wait."

"If that's the case, it doesn't look like Gertrude is going to happen today," Sue joked. "So, I'll leave you two at it. I'll be getting back to where the air's a bit sweeter."

"Thank you, Sue. It was thoughtful of you to think of us, sweltering in here," I said.

"If you miss the smell and get a hankering," David winked, "The door is always open."

The remaining crate had some interesting parts. We could only guess what they might be. David stretched. "There," he said, "another item to check off the list. All crates emptied. I think I'll call it a day. Prince is panting. He needs some fresh air. Do you want to come to the beach with us?"

This came as a surprise. He had never invited me before, and although I had reservations, wanting to keep our relationship a working-only thing, I said, "Why not? I could use some sea air, or is this an April Fool's Day prank?"

"Not at all," he said. "I wasn't even aware of the date. I thought you might want to get out of here. My gosh, we've been working on Gertie over a month. Bring a jacket. It's chilly by the sea."

When we walked across the parking lot, he pointed to a snazzy-looking red sports car.

"Yeah," I said, "I've seen it here before. I've wondered who owns such an expensive car."

"Oh? It's a Ferrari California 30 Gran Turismo." He opened the passenger door, and bowed with a smirk. "If you don't mind, Princess, please get in before it turns into a pumpkin."

"You've got to be kidding!" I said.

The wind tussled my hair.

"Relax. Breathe in the fresh air. Pretend you're a kid and you've run away from school."

"Ooof!" I exclaimed, to be heard over the wind. He drove far above the speed limit. "You're nuts," I raised an eyebrow. "Why do you own such an exotic car?"

"It feels less like an object to me and more like a reflection of who I am: an engineering man with good taste. Initially, she wasn't meant for city driving. She's been tamed, but I take her to the track and do tarmac-destroying test drives. I could buy two if I didn't have to pay so many speeding tickets. The police target this car, I'm sure of that."

Men and their toys! He's high and low, swinging between emotions. Could he be manic?

The drive to the beach twisted and turned down-hill. White-knuckled, I clung to the support rung. Thank God, the distance was short. "Well, here we are." He pulled into the sea-walk parking lot. "Imagine that," he said, "nary a ticket. Your hair must have frightened them off. Let's go down to the beach."

It sounded more like a command than an invitation. That and his haircut piqued a thought. *Has he been in the forces? Has that experience caused him to disguise an inner uncertainty by outwardly projecting the mien of a man in control? Or so it seems, at times, a bully?*

We took off our shoes, running bare foot in the sand. He showed me how to throw sticks for Prince to retrieve. I frolicked in the froth, laughing. I felt so carefree. This must be what a happy childhood felt like. It reminded me of coming to this very same beach with Grampa Y, kicking the same froth, feeling his love.

Then, without explanation, David went sprinting down the beach, leaving me alone. Prince followed him. *Why did he invite me just to leave me stranded?* I noticed how easily he ran. His entire body moved in rhythm, not unlike a gazelle.

I sat on the driftwood where I had left my jacket. Being still, I felt the chill and wrapped it around my shoulders. Bigger thoughts came to me. *With all his strangeness, why have I begun to like him? What is it that intrigues me? Why do I still have him hanging around? Might he be dangerous? Am I the one that's nuts?*

Those questions had me taking a sharp look at myself. Where am I in my life? Am I living the life that I want?

This was fun, I thought. *When did I last have fun?*

I remember running and hiding in the bushes behind Father's tukul, kicking a bladder ball with the other children.

The training in midwifery that I had in the Sudan hospital, although brief, was wonderful. For the first time in my life, I felt a belonging to something useful. Oh, the joy of catching a newborn. Even the thought of it still sends shivers up my spine. I remember the camaraderie of the women in that ward. Although they spoke different dialects, communication wasn't a problem. They gestured, they smiled, they laughed, and they danced. But most poignantly, we cried together with the mother when a baby died. It's no wonder I was torn between staying in South Sudan or going to Sweden.

When I was first here, my adopted family homeschooled me. What a difficult student I must have been. I was at the age when my wild hormones and having my family of origin ripped from me had me in constant crisis mode. It didn't help that I felt my language, the last hold I had to my identity, was being taken away. My adopted parents, doing everything they could think of to help, enrolled me in swimming lessons. It was so much fun. I felt a belonging to the group of kids, as we supported each other at competitions. I took art classes and discovered I had a talent. I enjoyed it so much; I would have spent my every waking hour painting if I had a choice. These activities got me out of the house and into the community. I took the bus to help me be independent and to become acquainted with the city.

When I moved out of the family home and into a turret, I found joy in decorating my own place. Living alone fed my independence. That's when I decided to study and have a career. I framed and hung the Maya Angelou quote on the wall next to the window where I often stand looking to the stars, meditating. "The better you know, the better you go." I worked hard and obtained a degree in interior design. It gave me a feeling of accomplishment.

Then, the family offered me the job as overseer of The Store—in charge of the finances, directing the design department, marketing, resourcing personnel. The confidence the family showed in me was a marker in making me feel grown up and responsible. Life was good.

But things have changed over time.

Was it burnout?

Was it because I have fallen into the habit of using productivity and money to decide whether something is worth doing?

Was it the problem I had with male and potential lover relationships?

I only know that I'm not happy.

I thought having Gertrude would put the joy back in my life, but she has come with problems. Not the least of which is David. If I'm honest,

I know I'm attracted to him beyond an employee/employer relationship. This should be scary enough to put an end to him, the sooner the better. Why should I wait until, like all my other male relationships, I frighten him off? Am I so desperate for romantic love that I can't decide what to do?

That most memorable line in William Wordsworth's *Daffodils* came to me, "—the inward eye which is the bliss of solitude."

Perhaps, I need to get away, take a holiday, lie in the sand in Hawaii, swim in the warm waters.

My thoughts turned to a book I'd just read by Kathleen Winter— *Undersong*. She tells us that because William had impaired hearing and sight, he depended on his sister Dorothy's insights of nature. Without her he was impotent, creatively speaking. It is hard for me to get my mind around that—all those enlightened words I've read did not truly belong to William Wordsworth. Unbelievable.

Maybe, no one puts their true self out for others to see. Perhaps, I'm not seeing the real David. More than likely, he has no idea who I truly am.

Sitting here, doing nothing, is frivolous and probably more than a bit crazy. Usually, I would chastise myself for wasting time but somehow, today it feels good.

Why do my insides feel lit up?

Why do I feel happy?

Why should I question?

David and Prince were now on the final stretch back.

Will I ever get to the bottom of who he is?

Do I really care to? Truth be told, I'm welcoming the distraction from my habitual life.

"You remind me of Copenhagen's *The Little Mermaid*," he said as he came up to me.

"How so?" I asked.

"A fish out of water becoming human."

"What do you mean?" It was a strange thing for him to say.

"I mean you look lovely." He grinned. "Now, it's time to get you back."

It seemed that he was dissecting me, then sugar coating it with a flirtatious compliment. I hope I didn't give him the satisfaction of a blush.

When he dropped me back at The Store, Sue and Monica were locking up. They waved, each one vying for David's attention. He was a welcome attraction, being the only male who worked on the premises. A handsome fit stud, and he was aware of all the sighing daisies.

"Nice car," Sue, the only one who had spoken with David, said.

"I love you too," David answered, winking. He was edging his way into their circle, flirt by flirt.

"I'll come back in a couple of days," he said to me. "Don't touch Gertie until I come. Later." He waved, and the Ferrari took off, leaving a flush of excited ladies in its wake.

Why has Gertrude now become his? I'll touch her if I please. He might be in command of the work on her but she's still mine. I'll not be pushed around.

When Karen, Grampa Y's wife, started The Store, she nailed a huge wooden header over the door. On it she had wood-burned:

Truth Goodness Unity Justice Beauty Love

These words are the guiding principles that we still try to follow. When I witness the natural camaraderie of the people who work here, I look up and give Gramma Karen a smile.

I sense that David is building his bridge into their embrace cautiously. His flirting, like he did with me on the day I met him, is how he handles awkward situations. He only flirts with me now when he's trying to dig his way out of becoming too emotional. Perhaps he thinks that flirting keeps everything light and superficial. And I have a strong feeling that he wants to belong to The Store group but has a fear of being rejected. It makes me wonder what has happened in his past that has such a strong influence on him.

I said goodnight to the girls and danced down the path from The Store to my turret. The iberis bushes showed white, the first to come out of hibernation. A chorus of croci poked up their heads, surveying the new world they entered. I performed a pirouette in their honor. My antique loom is like autumn leaves clinging to a tree, calling out, wanting to be useful again. *David, I'm sure we'll make her wish come true.*

Feeling positive, I went to work on the header that I was going to nail over the door of Gertrude's Place.

Fruitful Stewardship of Nature
Co-operation Accessibility Affordability Friendship

Scene Five
Coffee Mugs

We were having coffee in the kitchen. David was busy with the inventory ledger, checking off the parts that had arrived for the loom. He set down his pencil, looked up and said, "Have I told you how amusing it is that you cuddle your mug?"

"Yes, many times and I've told you how much I enjoy doing it."

"Well, as we are talking about coffee mugs…"

"I wasn't aware that we were talking about coffee mugs."

"Fiza, don't interrupt. I'm trying to make a point."

"I'm all ears."

"Your mugs are such an odd, mismatched assortment. Did your family members donate all their leftovers? I would gladly gift you a matching set. Tall ones, with circular rings in red. They would look great lined up in the glass cupboards, sparkling clean. Disorganization indicates a messy mind."

He must have been thinking about having this conversation for some time. He's even thought about the color.

"Hold on. Hold on," I said. "You get so carried away. You crack me up. It's amazing how our conversations can veer off course. We were discussing loom parts and for some strange reason it led to talking about my mugs."

"That's what I like about us," he said. "No subject is out of bounds."

"Well then, let me tell you something. Those so called mismatched mugs are a Storied Collection."

"There's one thing I've learned about you, Fiza."

"And what might that be?"

"You can justify anything. Just admit your mugs are an eyesore."

"Each mug has its own size, shape, color, history, and unique aura. I choose a different one based on the tone I want to set for the day ahead. They make me think of the people who gave them to me, the place where I bought them. This one for today was given to me by the girls in The Store when we had the opening of the Spring Collection. It represents good wishes, hope for success, friendship."

"You're dippy," he said, in a light joking manner.

Reminiscing felt good and I went on to say, "You know that big round one painted a yellow orange? An owner of a café at the head of Lake Como in Italy gave it to me. It reminds me of her beautiful generosity and the big round Tuscan sun. It warms me. We had climbed from her café up a winding trail so she could show me a spectacular view over the lake. To thank her, I gave her a small silk scarf from The Store. In return, she gave me a mug. We've kept in touch. We're planning to meet in Cortina, a quaint town on a hill in Tuscany that she wants to show me."

He listened, seeming to enjoy my tale, then said, "A canteen tin or a queen's porcelain cup deliver the same goods."

"Maybe so," I said, "but oh, the difference!" To further the conversation and to get to know him better, I asked, "Tell me something, David, do you make your bed every morning?" I had read that it tells a lot about a person's character if they make their bed every morning.

"Of course, a dime can bounce off it. I'm army trained. I'm regimented in everything I do."

"I rest my case."

"Not on my neatly fluffed pillowcase," he retorted, laughing.

Scene Six

The Turret

We worked for days on the harness frame, removing bent heddles, straightening those that were recoverable and replacing missing ones. It was important to have a perfectionist's bent when it came to heddles. The shuttle wouldn't pass backwards and forwards across the loom if they weren't uniform. I was pleased about our progress, so instead of taking a coffee break, I asked, "Would you like to go for a walk to my turret? I have iced tea and ginger snaps. Are you up for that?"

"Sounds good," David said, slipping out of his working smock. "I would like to see how a princess lives in a turret."

"Why do you refer to me as a princess?" I asked. "You've done it a couple of times."

"Why did I name my dog Prince?" he answered. "Because he's male and handsome."

"What's that to do with your calling me Princess?" I asked as we walked down the path to my turret.

"Because you're female and beautiful."

"You're incorrigible." As an introduction to my place, I said, "I've tried to elevate the sense of history that the turret has rather than erase it."

"Don't tell me," he said, "let me see it with fresh eyes. I hate it when someone recommends a movie then goes on to tell me what it's all about."

As we climbed the steep, three flights of outside stairs, he said, "These remind me of fire escapes. You have a built-in gym; no wonder you are so fit."

"Before I moved in, Dad had all the old electrical wiring replaced. The turret is up to date in that respect. Hopefully, I won't need to escape from fire." We arrived at the door. "It's the original door and I haven't changed the lock." I reached behind a wall plant of ivy and purple coleus and retrieved the over-sized key. Once inside, he glanced around. "Well," I asked, "what is your first impression?"

"I say that it doesn't look like a family home. And it doesn't appear to be trendy. You've personalized the space. From the little I know about you, I would guess that this is your stamp."

"I had a blank canvas. I wanted the pale walls to be an antidote for the noise of daily life."

"But the African Batik wall hanging is anything but pale; it stands out."

"I didn't say that I wanted it to be dull," I said. "Come, let me give you the five-minute tour."

In the skinny bathroom with all its bright, star-shaped, twinkling lights, David put his hand up to shade his eyes. "I'm blinded," he said, laughing. "How could I ever find the toilet?"

"I'm sure you would feel your way, if it was urgent enough," I answered, catching his mood. I thought the bathroom was enchanting. It was fun seeing it from a man's point of view.

"Now that my eyes have adjusted to the brightness," he said, "I can see the intriguing vanity mirror. Its amorphic form looks like it's framed with a necklace of colored glass shards."

"And it is. I'll show you my glass collection when we come to it."

We eased our way into the one-man kitchen. "I love to cook," he said. "It would be a challenge, but I would like to cook you a meal here. Is that being too presumptuous?"

"Not at all. I'll take you up on that, sometime," I answered, a little side-swiped by his remark.

"What berries are those in the colander?" he asked. "Are they for eating or are they art?"

"Red currants. I'm going to make jelly. If I'm successful and it sets, I'll bring a jar for The Store fridge. You can help yourself and let me know what you think."

"Homemade jelly. Yum! I can hardly wait."

We moved around the counter that separated the kitchen from the sitting room-cum-bedroom. He lingered, looking at the books that filled the shelves. "Your interests appear eclectic," he said. "Anna Karenina. Wuthering Heights. Celtic Spirituality." Then, he noticed my glass collection. All the tints of the rainbow were glinting from the shelf. "These are beautiful," he said, "and you've placed them in a perfect spot. I like the way the sun plays on them and reflects the colors around the room."

"Can I tell you their story?"

"Please."

"Before Mom left home to go to Medical School, Grandma took her for a holiday in Hawaii. They went to a Glass Beach. A sign read: It's against the law to remove the glass pieces from the beach."

"Don't tell me they absconded with these beauties illegally?"

"Yes, they did. They later found out that many tourists did the same. The woman who owns the gift shop by the beach has parcels coming in the mail without end. Tourists, whose conscience get the best of them, return the glass."

"And your mother and grandma? Didn't it bother them?" he asked.

"It bothered them, but they decided to gift me the glass and let me decide what should be done."

"And?"

"I'm thinking about it. I would like to go to Glass Beach and return them with ceremony. So?" I spread my arms wide, meaning to take in the entire space, "What do you think?"

"It's pretty."

"Pretty?"

"It's... cute."

"Cute?"

"You have an eye for design. You've made this space emotionally interesting with the batik African women, the Maya Angelo plaque, and the Hawaiian glass pieces, but I feel like an elephant trapped in a church bell tower. I wouldn't fit through that lone window if I wished to escape."

"We are three stories up." I laughed. "I wouldn't recommend the leap. Have a seat. I'll bring the iced tea."

"Seat?" he asked, looking around. "I haven't seen a bed, a table, or anything resembling a chair."

"The cushions on the floor are for sitting. Stretch your legs. I'll be right back."

"I like it," he said, as I sat and handed him his drink and offered the ginger snaps. "From the floor, your place feels warm and welcoming. You've bounced the colors off the African Batik, spread them around. They lead the eye, so one takes in the entire area–the yellow teakettle, the orange frame on the plaque over the door, the same colors repeated on the multi-colored counter base. I would say, tiny but lovely."

"Thank you, David. I'm aware that it reflects who I am, but I don't want it to feel pretentious. I would like my visitors to feel comfortable here."

"What do you do with that contraption when you have visitors?" He gestured to the apparatus I use to hang up-side-down that leaned against a wall. It is part of many 'self-help' routines.

"Oh, that. As you can see, I don't have a bed to slide it under. It's a little more difficult to disguise than my yoga mats. Most visitors want to give it a try. Are you game?"

"No. But I'm game to try these miniature, heart-shaped cookies. They smell delicious. Yummy." He smacked his lips after he had popped a few into his mouth. "You've sprinkled them with sugar. Spicy with a splash of sweet." I wondered if he was, in a roundabout way, describing me. "This has been a delightful break, but I want to finish with the heddles, today. We should be getting back," he said.

On our way out, he stopped and read the plaque over the door. "Happiness is not a goal. It's a by-product of a life well lived."—Eleanor Roosevelt.

"I like that," he said.

Scene Seven
Lunch at the Beach House

W e went for lunch at a café that overlooked the sea. I had never been here. David had described its nautical atmosphere, and he was so right. The walls were painted so you felt like you were dining in a huge wave tunnel. We toasted each other with a cold frothy glass of beer, then dug into the attractive aromatic offerings the waiter had set before us. A creamy mustard sauce gave the sil, a local fish, just the right amount of tang. The hard-boiled egg slices complemented the colours and gave a different texture. We sopped up the extra sauce with chunks of fresh rye bread. "You're dripping it down your chin," David said, laughing, as he leaned over and wiped me clean. In the middle of this, David asked, "When is your birthday?"

"I don't know," I said.

"What do you mean you don't know? Everyone knows their birthday."

"My adoption papers state that I was born in the spring. On the first day of spring, Dad would make a big deal, taking the calendar from the fridge door, finding a pen, asking what day I would like to celebrate my birthday. When I had decided, he marked the date with a big X. It made me feel special. My siblings had a set date; they didn't have a choice."

"Interesting," he said. "Have you always known that you were adopted?"

"I was about twelve or thirteen when Dad and I went to the adoption center in South Sudan. He wanted to bring me to Sweden. At that time, Mom was already in Sweden, so she adopted me later."

"That sounds like a thousand-pieced puzzle, and none of the pieces are bled from the same die. There's never anything simple about you.

You're so complicated. I'll need to stretch out my time working on the loom if I'm ever to figure you out. Let's take our beers and sit out on the bench."

"Is that an invitation or a command? Your army training affects how you treat me, do you realize that?"

"I meant it as an invitation. Thanks for bringing me up short. I haven't had training in how to treat a lady."

"You're welcome, and yes, I would like to go sit in the sun."

The sea reflected the azure-blue cloudless sky. Its beauty made me think that David and I were clearing our clouds and the foundation of our relationship was firming up.

"You might say that my family life was defined by absence," David said.

This took me by surprise. I thought we would continue talking about me. Didn't he say that he was trying to figure me out?

What could I say? I waited to see if he might add something or leave it at that.

He looked out over the water and drank his beer. "Our house was filled with sadness, alcohol, and violence," he continued.

The rote-like tone made it sound like he had told this story many times, perhaps only in his head. I knew how debilitating that could be. I had recited, in my head, my sad childhood over and over, until my adopted mom helped me get my story out of my head and down on paper. Perhaps I'm David's paper.

"When my mother was home, which was seldom, she was withdrawn. The only time Father interacted with me was when he took me to Science World, on occasion. We would tinker together, trying to figure out how things worked. I remember taking apart a watch and putting it back together. It amazed me that when we had finished, it worked. Another time, we took apart an old radio, and when we put it back together, it functioned much better than before we worked on it."

I said, "Oh, that's probably why you like tinkering with Gertrude."

He either didn't hear or ignored me.

"It wasn't until I was about twelve that I learned the source of my family's dysfunction and sorrow."

He hesitated, snapped his fingers for the wandering waiter to bring him another beer. He didn't ask if I wanted one. It was as if I wasn't there, and he was talking to the sea.

"I had an older sister. She was six. I was four."

He clenched his fists. Every muscle tensed. His face became a distorted ugly mask.

He frightened me–his appearance, his obvious anger. I contemplated either standing up and walking away or silently waiting. The latter won, probably because I was moved by a flood of empathy. I put my hand on his arm.

In a few moments, I felt him relax.

"Sorry," he said. "I thought it no longer had a hold on me."

"It's alright, David," I said, "you don't need to tell me. Maybe some other time."

"No Fiza, this is the closest I've come to telling anyone. Please, let me tell you."

"If you wish," I said.

"She ran out into the street, chasing a butterfly. A car hit her. All I can remember is Mother screaming. All these years, and Mother's screams still wake me."

I wiped away the tears that rolled down his face.

"Thank you," he whispered. "You've found my laugh lines and my scars." He took my hand, kissed my palm, and said, "I made peace with my wrinkles and scars when I was practicing self-acceptance."

"Then why the shadow beard?" I asked.

"Some scars are harder to make peace with," he said, "but that's another story."

He took out his wallet. "I carry a picture of my sister. Would you like to see it?"

"Yes, I would like that. What is her name?"

"Elaine." He handed me a well-creased photo.

A little girl with a big bow in her curly black hair wore a pink party dress. White socks came to her knees and her feet were tucked into shiny, black leather shoes. A big smile filled her face. "She's beautiful," I said. "She looks so bright-eyed and curious like her brother."

"I often wonder what she would have become and how life might have been different if she had lived. But she didn't. And the pain of losing her ruined my parents. It destroyed our family."

For a moment, I thought of my African siblings, and I had difficulty suppressing the tears that were threatening to escape. I was thankful when David continued to speak.

"I always had an innate curiosity. A strong desire to reach out and touch the unreachable. That's why I knew I had to get an education. Without one, my dreams would remain only dreams. I can't imagine what would have become of me in that dead-end, down-trodden town. But when the time came for me to go to college, there wasn't any money. I joined the US Forces. The army paid for my education. I'm an engineer, thanks to them. I enjoyed the army's basic training; it felt good being fit. After basics, the stealth exercises and the shooting range fascinated me. I considered sniper training. I spent every chance I got at the range and became an excellent shot." He raised his arms as if he were shooting a rifle. "Pow pow. Pow pow. Pow, pow, pow. There. I've shot all the bad things from my childhood away. Thanks to you, I'm able to let go. I don't need them anymore. You have such a kind heart, Fiza. Such a generous spirit."

"Thank you, David, but, as you know, I'm not all softness. You've witnessed many of my other faces."

He jumped up and said, "Here's a plan. Let's pick up Prince and our swimsuits and go for a swim in the sea. What do you say?"

"It's still April. It'll be cold. What the heck. I could use a cooling off. Why not?"

I had much to ponder. His pow powing, pretending to shoot, was scary. His sudden mood swings alarmed me, but I concentrated on the current plan. I had many swimming lessons, entered many competitions, but I had never swum in the sea.

When we were driving, he said, "It surprises me that I didn't study to become a pilot. I dream of soaring to places that have not yet been seen."

"You may not have become a pilot but when you drive Miss Ferrari, you're like a hang glider, bouncing off the cliffs," I said.

"Do I frighten you?"

"It did at first, but not anymore. It's exhilarating."

"I didn't become a pilot. I've never glided, but you lift me to great heights," he said, pressing a heavy foot on the gas pedal. He gave me a quick glance, and I caught the twinkle in his dark eyes. He was enjoying himself.

I don't know if it was him being a dare-devilish driver, squealing the tires on the corners or our talk about flying to great heights, but the Greek legend of Icarus came to me. I didn't know if he was up on Greek legends, but I asked, "Are your wings made of wax?"

"I love your quick retorts. I trust you'll keep me from flying too close to the sun."

He *was* up on Greek legends.

In the sea, the water would be cold. We frolicked and splashed each other while running close to the shore, trying to adjust our body temperatures. Prince barked at the shore birds, as he ran beside us. Then we took the plunge. We swam, stroke for stroke, far out. I was pleased that all my swimming classes hadn't been for naught, and I was in sync with this fit man.

We paused and treaded water for a while. David came close and lifted strands of hair off my face. "I love your wet hair," he commented. "It's curlier."

"Thank you, David, for suggesting this. It's just what I needed. I didn't realize that I was missing the water. I feel washed clean."

"So do I," he said. "Race you back."

"To be fair, I'll give you a head start," I answered.

We side kicked back, facing each other, chatting.

Prince saw us coming, gave up his shore bird barking, and swam out to meet us.

On the ride back to The Store, David asked, "We had fun, didn't we?"

"Didn't we just," I said.

Scene Eight
Post-Traumatic Stress Disorder

For a May afternoon it was unbearably hot. We opened all the windows in Gertrude's Place and set up fans where we worked, but nothing seemed to help. Our clothes stuck to us and sweat ran down our faces, blurring vision. We were attaching tiny parts in difficult to get at places on the loom. Having to stop and wipe away the sweat was frustrating. David was short with me, and he slammed away at his tools. I realized he was irritated. He sets progress goals and because of the heat, we weren't meeting his expectations. Taking command, I said. "Let's call it a day." I set down my wrench, climbed out from under the loom, stretched, and headed for the kitchen.

"Take out a cold beer for me, please. I'll be right there. Just give me a minute to put things away," David called.

It wasn't any cooler in the kitchen, but the cold beer was refreshing. We were relaxed, listening to a woodpecker knocking on the maple just outside the window. Ever since our lunch at the Beach House and our swim together, we seemed to have a better understanding of each other. He had taken to heart my, *is that a command or an invitation*, and tried to be sensitive to my feelings. Working together became much more pleasant.

"This heat takes me back to Iraq," David said. "The worst heat I've ever encountered was in Fallujah. It was blistering hot, and a desert dust hovered over everything, making an already difficult mission impossible. And it wasn't much better in Afghanistan. The heat..." David stood, put his arms around me and pulled me to the floor. Holding me, he yelled, "Tim. Oh Tim, they got you. No Tim. No. No. No. Oh my God Tim.

No. No. No. Tim. Tim, can you hear me? Tim don't go. Tim don't go. Oh my god, Tim. Please don't go. Please don't leave me."

He dropped me and fell across my body, sobbing. I was terrified. *Was he going to harm me?* Try to think, I told myself. He had me pinned. I smelled urine. *Had I wet myself? How can I get him off me? How can I get away?* I couldn't move. I spent what seemed like an eternity yelling out to him, begging him to get off, calling to Grampa for help. Hoarse and shaking, I felt him stir. He got up, leaving me on the wet floor. I heard the door slam.

Days passed. He didn't come back. I thought I had seen the last of him.

What had happened played over and over in my mind. I couldn't sleep because I tried to understand, to figure it out. Because David had been talking about his deployments, I concluded it had to do with his war experiences, but I had never seen anyone react like he did. The fear I felt while he pinned me down would suddenly flood over me. I wasn't eating properly, staring into space with my fork in the air. I became shaky, on edge.

When I explained what had happened to Dad, he told me something that I was totally unaware of. "Fiza," he started, "I was a doctor in South Sudan. Terrorists kidnapped me and took me to their camp to treat their leader who had been shot. That's where I met you. You, along with a few other young girls, assisted me. Although I was there to help, I was treated horrendously by the boy-soldiers. It was as if they didn't want their leader to survive, and they tried everything to incapacitate the doctor. You came to my aid on many occasions. I know you were sneaking food for me, even going hungry to feed me."

"Dad," I said, "I have no memory of being in that camp. I only remember escaping, thrashing through the bushes, trying to find my village."

"The point of my telling you this is because I suffered from the trauma of that experience. I had episodes like you have just described David having. There's a medical term for it. It is called Post-Traumatic Stress Disorder. David needs help. Is he under psychiatric care?"

"I don't know. I don't think he'll come back," I said.

"If he does, tell him that I would like to share my experience with him. I would like him to know that I care."

"Thank you so much, Dad," I said, hugging him tight. "I wish I had come sooner. I feel such relief. I'll wait a while, to see if David comes back, before looking for someone else to help me with Gertrude."

I now understood why Hegel, the great German philosopher who is often called the foundation figure of Modern philosophy, likened a mysterious feeling to the Owl of Minerva, which according to Greek legend, "takes its flight only when the shades of night are gathering," which is to say, we only understand a moment in our lives when it has passed. Dad had helped me understand. I now felt like I could face life like normal again.

A month passed. One morning when I went to stock the kitchen, there he was. The new picking sticks had arrived, and he was unwrapping them. He looked up, "Oh, there you are," he said. "Sue let me in. You're late. Coffee's getting cold."

No one had warned me he'd be here. I had trouble finding words. "Oh... thank you, David," I managed and started towards the kitchen, knees weak, gut clenching.

My shaking hands made it difficult to get a steady cup to my mouth, but I persisted, thinking that the warm coffee might help. I was freezing.

What now?

Do I wait for him to come and give me an explanation?

Should I just go out and start to work, as if nothing had happened?

Maybe I should climb out the window and run away.

This is all too complex.

I chastised myself, put on my smock and walked to the work floor.

"Faint of heart, I am not," I whispered, repeatedly.

I stood beside him and said, "David, we need to talk."

"I'm sorry," David said, "I know I had an episode. I don't know exactly how it went, but I felt the horrible pain of it. When I left, I went to see my psychiatrist. She explained that I probably have these episodes because I have buried trauma that I couldn't handle, deep in my memory. Something triggers the memory, and I relive the trauma. 'Feeling the pain,' the psychiatrist said, 'will help you let the memory go.' I don't know, Fiza, how much more needs to come out. I just want you to know I'm truly sorry you had to witness that."

"I understand," I said. "I've spoken to Dad about it." I then told him Dad's story, and mentioned that Dad would be open to share more experiences with him.

"I would like that," he answered. "The psychiatrist tells me, to heal, I need to talk about things that happened to me. That I must stop keeping horrible things hidden."

Scene Nine
David and My Family

D avid and Dad met many times over the next couple of months. Dad told me that David is curious about many things. "He's been asking how I feel about abortions. He wants to know my opinion on doctor assisted suicide. He's a delight. He lets me drive the Ferrari." But Dad never mentioned if he and David had discussed Post-Traumatic Stress Disorder. What was private between them, he kept private.

It was during these months that David got to know my family. We often had impromptu gatherings at Mom and Dad's, at the turret, or at David's apartment. He and Mom ended up in the kitchen cooking. I loved hearing them chatter away.

One time, I overheard this conversation. "Mrs. Doc," David said. "Taste the sauce. Does it need more spice?"

"It's perfect," Mom answered, "Our tastebuds have become more Swedish than Sudanese. And Ellie can come. She especially can't take too much heat."

"Which Ellie do you mean? I never know if the family is referring to the aunt in Ireland or Fiza's sister. It's quite confusing for an outsider."

"If we mean the Ellie in Ireland, we'll say Aunt Ellie. The children say Grand Aunt Ellie. Gramma Tree usually calls her by her full name, Ellie Mae. She's Gramma Tree's sister. My daughter, Ellie, is coming for dinner."

"I'm glad Ellie can come for dinner. I only met her that once when she dropped by when I was visiting Mr. Doc. She's got a lot of spunk,"

David said. "She's so much like Fiza. I'm looking forward to getting to know her, and I would like to meet her brothers."

"Paul is doing an exchange year in England and Chriz is still in the US. They come home when they get a chance, usually seldom. If you think the Ellie thing is strange, when he was little, we called Chriz Patrick, Pat, but when he was a teenager, he wanted to be called Chriz. So, he gets Pat or Chriz. There I've straightened out one more puzzle for you."

"Or added to it. Anyway, while Ellie's home, I would like to treat everyone to an evening at the Karaoke Café."

"That would be wonderful, David. She's back to Ireland on Monday. Maybe we can go this weekend? Mr. Doc has a marvelous voice. We don't get to hear it enough."

"Fiza told me that Ellie goes to your alma mater, the Medical School at Trinity College. You must be proud of her."

"Did you know that after Medical School I joined a charity group, Doctors Without Borders, and was posted to the hospital in Juda, South Sudan? That's where I met Mr. Doc."

"Please, Mrs. Doc, would you sit down with me sometime and fill things in. I have a thousand questions."[1]

"It would be my pleasure, David. I like talking about my interesting family. One day, when you and Mr. Doc come back from the racing track, you and I will watch him wash the Ferrari, and I'll answer your questions. But now, let's serve dinner."

---

[1] Marlene F Cheng, The Madam's Friend, If the reader is confused may I suggest they read this book. It gives details about Tijay (Mom, Mrs. Doc) at Trinity College, going to South Sudan, marrying Dr. Z. (Mr. Doc) and how they adopted Fiza and came back to Sweden. Ellie their daughter was born in South Sudan. They have two sons, Paul and Chriz, who were born in Sweden.

Scene Ten

I was holding my phone when I saw it light up. It was David. *Why would he be texting me this late*?

Princess do ya wanta watch the sunset?

OK.

I'll pick you up in 10.

Princess? I shouldn't balk. He probably means it as an endearment.

We found our spot by the driftwood, and he spread out a gigantic blanket.

"Army surplus?" I laughed, sat on the blanket, and leaned against the log.

"No, Gertie wove it just for us," he said.

We still didn't know if Gertrude would ever weave, but his positive thinking felt good.

"This is perfect," I commented. "The sky is smiling sapphire. Warm breeze. Nothing to do but wait for the twilit colours to end a well spent day. I'm pleased that both harness frames are up. Gertrude is beginning to look like a loom. I'm so excited."

"And the reed frame is ready to be installed. My next job is to check the cloth rolls and figure out where and how they should be attached," he said. "Don't get too excited. It's going to be a while yet. I knew we would have a wait before the sun set, so I brought us drinks. He opened the bottles, using the cap of one to flip the cap of the other. "A true Heineken," he said, handing me one. "None of that diluted stuff for *my* princess."

He's sure in a bouncy mood, I thought.

He sat close beside me, Prince curled up at our feet.

"Skal."

"Skal."

He leaned into me. I felt him through our summer clothing. Any personal time we spent together, away from work, was becoming more and more enjoyable. Feeling his body next to mine gave me a sense of security. I wondered what it would be like to have him for a life-partner. Whatever that might mean. *How do you feel?* I asked myself. *Content,* I answered. *Happy. Is this what love feels like?* I sipped the cold beer, lost in thought.

David brought me back to the present by saying, "Your hair smells like sweet honeysuckle in bloom. It reminds me of home."

"A good memory, I hope."

"One of few."

"How so?"

"I spent two years in Iraq on different missions. After Iraq, I was deployed to Afghanistan with six of my closest mates. Only three of us came back," he said, focusing on the sea.

"I'm so sorry, David," I said.

"And two that came back committed suicide."

My hands flew up to my mouth. "Sorry," I whispered.

The pleasant evening vanished. It seemed as if black clouds had rushed in, pressing down on me. Spasms of pain shot through my guts. I swallowed hard to keep the vomit down.

"Soldiers are supposed to be battle-hardened. We should be resilient and unaffected emotionally, but we are human.

"Each death I saw took a part of me. Death scenes haunted my nightmares, had me waking up screaming. Fear of the nightmares had me forcing myself to stay awake. Exhausted, I would fall asleep when I was standing guard or driving a tank. I was a danger to myself and my comrades.

"My mates' suicides affected me even more than the deaths I had witnessed in battle. On top of the debilitating grief, I felt an all-consuming guilt. Why didn't I see it coming? Why hadn't I been there for them? We had each other's backs in combat. Why had that not continued when we returned?

"I felt alone in a world that didn't understand me, and I lost the struggle to understand it.

"I wanted to shield people from war and the battle I was fighting once I came home. I had been regimental all my life. I believed I could get through this on my own.

"In my struggle, I became a lone wolf. Stopped caring about everything, including myself. I didn't want to eat. The bottle was my companion.

"I vowed never to let anyone close. If I let anyone in, I rationalized that they would die. Even the thought of it was too painful. That wasn't a road I was willing to re-take.

"I forced myself to become emotionally dead. I wasn't living; I was barely existing. Standing still. For the first time, I realized where nowhere is.

"I wondered if I was being rational, if maybe I had gone crazy. I gave in to the idea that you don't think rationally when bombs are exploding around you."

I stroked his arm. I felt when he tensed and when he released. It was like reading him in braille. I wanted to hold him close as I thought of kind words. Anything, to bring him back from his grey world.

Anything to give it color. But he never gave me space. Every time I tried to put an arm around him, he moved away. He wasn't allowing me in. A touch was as close as I could come.

"Fiza, can I tell you a story?" he asked. His tone lightened.

"What's that?" I asked, praying that it wasn't more darkness.

"When I first returned to the States, hockey players from the Washington NHL team visited veterans. A Swedish player and I hit it off.

"He would say, 'I admire your dedication to your country. You gave your all, trying to bring peace to the world. That's a great inspiration.'

"And I would answer him, 'I've followed you. You give your all to be the best hockey player that you can be. You inspire people to be passionate about what they do.'

"He and I talked a lot about sports, about life.

"God, I loved that man.

"He found me on the street when I was in a very bad way, and checked me into the army hospital. If anyone else had tried to take me to the hospital, I would have fought them. I respected him, so I went. I was diagnosed with Post-Traumatic Stress Disorder and had intensive treatment. The hospital saved my life for the second time."

He already knew that he suffered from PTSD.

"For the second time?" I asked. Since he was on a roll and because he had alluded to it, I thought he might tell me about the first time he had been saved.

"You've seen the scar under my beard and my leg sets off any security metal detector."

"What happened?"

"A roadside bomb. I was airlifted to Germany and flown home to the new Walter Reed in Bethesda, Maryland. Tim was flown home in an airbag. When I left the hospital, the army gave me my pink slip and a pension. What they didn't give me was a manual on how to live a civilian life."

"I hope military forces have become aware of their neglect and are improving how they take care of the soldiers that give so much," I said.

"When I left the hospital, after my second stay, even though I didn't feel like the person I once was—the soldier before I went to Iraq and Afghanistan—I decided that I would become a force to be reckoned with. I would become the me I wanted to be.

"I knew the memory of Afghanistan would never leave me, but I was determined to live without its interference. I told myself if I worked hard, I deserved to have the life that my hockey friend had. Money was the big thing. Lots of it. I wanted to afford designer cloths, expensive cars.

"Why must I understand my life? I kept telling myself. I must live it.

"I learned to cook and ate well. I joined a gym and hired a personal trainer. Started running. I was determined to become army-fit but to do it without more bodily harm."

"And look at you. You've most certainly been successful in that regard," I said.

"Army pension being what it is, I needed to get a job to finance this new-found expensive lifestyle. I yearned for a change of scenery, a new beginning. One day, I noticed an ad in a scientific magazine. An engineering company in Sweden was looking to hire. Because I had been away from engineering theory for five years, I wondered if I was pretending to know more than what I did, but finding confidence, I filled out the form and here I am."

"David," I said. "I'm speechless."

"I've kept my story in my head. The psychiatrist in the States and the one continuing my psychiatric care here have tried to help me speak about things, but the words are like tadpoles stuck in a pond of muck. They have encouraged me to re-live what happened. I can't do that. I don't want to revisit my wounds. That would de-rail me. But with you, Fiza, my words are becoming unstuck."

"Why is that?"

"Fiza, I don't have a why. It just spills out. I've tried hard to keep it in my past. To carry on as if it didn't happen. To be normal. But with you, keeping silent doesn't feel comfortable anymore. Maybe my subconscious feels that you understand. Fiza, I've never ever felt supported or that someone cared. I sense that from you. Somehow you can draw out my pain. You force me to look at it. You make me laugh. You make me cry. That's how powerful your pull is on me."

I felt his trembling and made every effort to steady myself not to let tears come. I asked, "What does it feel like to say it out loud?"

"Good."

"What can I do to help?"

"You've helped me remember. Now, I'm depending on you to help me forget."

He got up and ran down the beach. He appeared lighter. His rhythmic movements seemed to take him in flight. Prince followed.

His actions made me realize that every time he was getting emotionally close to me, he distanced himself.

At the point where the beach curves, they turned and started back.

Metaphorically, perhaps he didn't want me to lose sight of him, but I must remember that he doesn't want to get too close to anyone.

Where is the line?

When he reached me, he took me in his arms and rolled us in the blanket with only our heads sticking out. He whispered into my hair, "Perhaps this is fate. Perhaps you were born to lift my spirits and help me fly. I'm soaring."

How can he say such things after making it clear that he doesn't want to get emotionally close to me? I think he reacts naturally, and when he thinks about how he feels about me, he panics. What about my feelings? Does he ever stop to think that he keeps me in tumultuous turmoil?

The sun wept its colors into the sea's embrace. It surrendered and slipped beneath the horizon. Prince curled up at our feet. In the soft winds dancing through my hair, I thought I heard:

"Please don't ever leave me.

Please don't ever leave

Please don't ever

Please don't

Please..."

Why are the words coming to me and then disappearing one by one? Is this a precognition? Have I seen the full count of David? Will he now disappear, bit by bit? Is the last word, please, significant? In the end, will I be begging him to stay?

Scene Eleven

When I arrived at Gertrude's Place in the morning, David worked on the warper, attaching it in place on the frame. Sue must have unlocked the door for him. I barely got a nod. He didn't even return my, "Good morning, David." I started for the kitchen to hide out and soothe my bruised feelings.

"Come quickly!" he said. "Come."

Have I become his dog, having to obey his every command? I sauntered over.

"Here. Hold this. Line up the holes."

"Great," he said, fitting in the bolt and turning the nut. "That's good for now. I'll need you to do the same on the other end, later."

I picked up a manual on the warper and went to get coffee.

I must have gotten carried away reading and was probably gone longer than what David expected. I felt his presence. A hint of prickliness. A dash of daring. The full dollop of it demanded my attention. I knew he was there, but I was determined to ignore him, as he had ignored me earlier. But my resolve melted, and I raised my eyes. He leaned against the door frame, smirking. So reminiscent of the day I first met him. "Oh!" I said, feigning surprise. "Have you been waiting for me?"

"I've been studying you," he said. "You look as if you're dancing in wildflowers."

"How so?"

"Peony top. Poppy pants. Sun glistening off your hair. Has anyone ever told you you're beautiful?"

"Has anyone ever told you you're bonkers? Do come in. Sit down. You must need a coffee. I'll make you one."

"That would be nice, but can't you just say, 'Thank you, David, for the lovely compliment?'"

"Thank you, David, for the lovely compliment. Now, please sit down." I got up to make his coffee, looked at him and said, "After our talk last night and your silence this morning, I thought you were trying to distance yourself. I wouldn't have been surprised if you hadn't come today."

"Sorry. I was concentrating. The warper is more complicated than I had envisioned. Sometimes I get lost."

"We don't have conversations that wander off wherever they please when you're concentrating. I can tell when your head is overcrowded with thoughts, but this morning, I sensed a 'no trespassing' sign, written clearly across your face. Or maybe I was imagining things. I'm feeling overly sensitive after our evening on the beach."

His eyes were sad. After leaving the warper and coming to the kitchen, he had shifted from being closed and tight to approachable and gentle, even complimentary. I was sorry that I had over reacted. I didn't know what came over me. I kissed his cheek. "There," I said, "my compliment to you." He smiled ear to ear, and pointed at his other cheek. I obliged. "Now you owe me one." I laughed.

"That was like a flitting firefly," he said. "Couldn't you at least linger?"

"You're incorrigible, David." I started towards the coffee maker. When I glanced back, he was pointing at his closed eye lids, grinning. He was having fun being playful, trying to put a better start to the rest of the day.

"You've gone nuts," I said. "Even when you're losing, you think you're winning. What kinky egotism!" I placed two kisses where he wished them, then backed away before things got out of hand.

When I was making the coffee, he started to sing: "You froth my soul. Keep my heart on simmer..."

I hadn't seen this side of him. *How many different Davids are inside this man?*

While we drank our coffee, he said, "Fiza, I sense a loneliness in you. Something that matches my own. I want to know you. I want you to understand me. I've fought it for some time, but I've come to think, if we're working together, what harm can come from being friends?"

"None that I can think of," I answered. "Now, my friend, let's go see to the warper."

Scene Twelve
Heigh-Ho, Heigh-Ho, It's Off to Work I Go

Life became fun. Perhaps it had to do with Gertrude starting to look more like a loom than a collection of parts. She was becoming less of a puzzle. We had more grunt stuff and fewer head problems, so David wasn't always in deep concentration, and, while working, we often engaged in light, many faceted conversations, not unlike the ones enjoyed over coffee.

I remember when we adjusted waft wires, I stood to stretch out my back. I glanced at David. His head bounced up and down. "What's with the head dance?" I asked.

"I'm singing in my head."

"Oh?"

"Isn't it interesting how music defines a place," he stated.

"How so?" I asked.

"Take reggae for instance. Nothing says reggae like Jamaica.

"Apparently, in the early 60's it was called ska. It had a heavy four-beat rhythm."

"Has it always been about drums?" I asked, trying to remember reggae.

"Yes, but also guitars and the scraper."

"What's a scraper?"

"A corrugated stick that is rubbed by a plain stick.

"Their music expressed a defiant human spirit that refused to be suppressed. There was an uprising of the poor. They were rejecting white-man's culture—fighting for independence from Britain—and you could hear it in their music."

"Wow! You understand music and its ability to help people deal with their feelings." I said, trying to add to the conversation. I wondered if this reggae music fed his desire to have a financially independent life, so he wouldn't suffer like the dispossessed of Jamaica.

"Ska was eventually replaced with a sound called *skengway*. It was meant to better suit a rock market. I've read that the chunking sound that comes at the end of each measure represents gunshots ricocheting in the ghettos of Kingston."

I asked, "Why the word skengway?"

"Skeng means gun or ratchet knife. But that's enough about reggae. I was singing an ABBA song in my head," he said.

"A more cheerful one, I hope."

"Like I said earlier, music defines a place. I knew nothing much about Sweden, but my Swedish NHL hockey friend was always singing ABBA's 'The Winner Takes It All.' Sweden was defined for me by that song."

"Were you thinking about your friend? Is that what you were singing in your head?"

"No, I was switching between 'Dancing Queen' and 'Take a Chance on Me.'"

"Oh." I said, wondering if those songs had anything to do with me. I quickly added, "The only ABBA words that come to me are '*on top of the world looking down on creation*'."

"Really? I think your forte is swimming and decorating. Those words belong to a group called The Carpenters."

"Oh. How do you know so much about music?"

"It's a part of me," he answered, then sang:

Such a feelin's comin' over me
There is wonder in most everything I see
Not a cloud in the sky, got the sun in my eyes
And I won't be surprised if it's a dream..."

We ended the day on that high note.

I missed David on the days he didn't come to work, and had trouble concentrating, when catching up on tasks at The Store. I spent more time wandering from department to department, chatting with the girls, then with my nose in the books.

"Don't you look elegant," has become Sue's morning greeting.

"Thank you," I answer, and usually add, "My sweats are in the laundry."

In the design room, Monica asked, while holding up a piece of fabric, "What do you think?"

"I like it. The different shades of blue are perfect," I said. "Is this for our outdoor collection? I miss designing. Maybe, we can collaborate on something for the spring collection."

"Surely, you can think of something negative about it," she said, smiling. "What's up with you? You seem so bouncy."

"I wouldn't know, but the birds were singing so cheerfully on my way here. Maybe they set my mood."

"It's been a while," Monica said. "Do you have time to have coffee with us?"

"That would be nice. I'm tired of taking coffee at my desk, fretting over problems."

"You look so relaxed," Yonga, who does the window displays, commented. "Have you shifted your undying devotion from Gertrude to David?"

"When Gertrude's running, and it surely won't be long," I said, ignoring her question, "let's have a celebration party. Anna, you're the social organizer, you better start planning."

"A pub night?" she asked.

"Bigger than that. Dinner and beer, in the least."

"Will David come?" Monica asked.

"Of course," I said. "A petunia in an onion patch."

We all agreed what fun that would be.

Scene Thirteen
A Karaoke Date

David looked at me and said, "You probably think this is weird, but in some of my darkest hours I talk to Elaine and find comfort."

How does one answer that?

"Why would I think that's weird? You had a sister and she died. My Grandpa Y is dead, and I talk to him all the time. I tell him my problems. Just thinking that he's listening comforts me."

"Thank you for understanding. It means a lot to me. I haven't told anyone else. I guess I'm afraid they would think I was cuckoo." He changed the subject by saying, "I was uncomfortable with our role in Afghanistan. We had been there twenty years, and what had we accomplished? We pulled out. The Taliban took over. In my opinion, the Afghan people are worse off than before we interfered. And their beautiful country is in shambles. History, I'm certain, will show the tremendous impact of the errors and horrors of that war."

"I think about the women," I said. "If the news has it right, they are losing the few hard-fought freedoms they had slowly gained over the last two decades. Apparently, the new hardline Taliban leader has decreed that women can't appear in public unless only their eyes are visible—you know, the burka thing. And no schooling past the sixth grade. How horrible is that? It made me happy to hear that some women are being defiant. They reject the burka, wrap a big scarf over their heads, and only pull it up over their face if they sense danger. But they live in fear. If the Taliban decide that a woman is violating the dress code, they severely punish the men in their lives. I think the Taliban is purposefully trying to erase girls and women from public life. Their misogynistic ways are gender apartheid."

"I've been told that leader imposes a strict brand of Islam that is mixed with ancient tribal traditions," he said, "but I feel encouraged when people tell me there is dissention in the party, hard-liners against pragmatists. The party could fragment, then it will be anyone's guess where Afghanistan will head."

"People who can, are leaving," I added. "Probably the wealthy and the educated. I feel so sorry for that country."

"I'm not going to wait for the history books," he spoke softly. "The U.S. and other countries have a responsibility for the disaster that is now Afghanistan. And I refuse to feel powerless as an individual. However small, I intend to do something for the Afghan people that will have a more positive impact than I ever made as a soldier. The material things that I am gathering are an investment. Someday, I'll put their profit to good use."

He paused for a moment, and I waited for him to gather his thoughts. *I like this benevolent side of him.*

He sprang to his feet, and in a much louder and enthusiastic voice he asked, "Would you like to go out for dinner?"

I jumped at the sudden noise.

"We could go to the Karaoke Café, have dinner, then join the karaoke fun. What do you say?"

"I say that would be nice." I brushed back my hair, keeping my hands busy. This sudden shift from discussing Afghanistan to an invitation took me by surprise. I felt awkward. "Is this a date, then?" I managed.

"Yes," he said. "I'll pick you up at six. If I'm picking you up that makes it a date. I'm leaving now. See you then."

What does one wear to a Karaoke Café? I didn't have much time to shower and try on different looks, because before I knew it, precisely at six, I heard him bounding up the outside stairs to the door of my turret.

When I opened the door, there stood a handsome man in black. A slight show of the chest and a gold chain. Pressed trousers. Signature belt buckle. Polished Italian loafers. He always dressed smartly, but this seemed to be a particularly elegant version of David. Perhaps my excitement affected my vision.

"Is the Princess ready?" he asked. "Your hair is gorgeous. I won't put the top down and have it disassembled. Bring a sweater; the evening gets a bit chilly." I turned, twirling my skirt, and went to the closet to get a sweater. I felt like a ballerina. I wanted to leap into the air, become airborne— échappé sauté came to me.

"Wait," he said, "do that again."

"Do what?"

"Turn. Your skirt shimmers like clouds moving in the sun. You look divine."

"You're a bit handsome yourself. Chic with no socks."

"These loafers are soft. My bare feet like the feel."

We held hands and started down the outside stairs.

I noticed a Tudor watch. *More than just a time piece—expensive jewellery.*

A gentle whiff of Paco Rabanne flamed my senses, a squeeze of refreshing lemon.

These things made me think of the two most precious men in my life, Dad and Grampa Y. *Is that the attraction?*

"You're such a gentleman," I said.

"How's that?"

"You walk on the outside of the stairs and go before me."

"So?"

"In the olden days, men walked on the outside of the street to take the slops that might come down from above. They walked ahead of the lady on the stairs to catch her if she fell. You're so slick. You have this dating thing down to a science. You must be well practiced."

When we reached the landing, he stopped and took both of my hands. "Not in the least. I've learned, from experience, that confidence, independent of aptitude, breeds success."

"What do you mean?"

"I'm not charismatic. I'm introverted and shy. I don't know my way around women, but I've learned that showing confidence, even when it's totally lacking, does wonders for my ability to handle awkward situations."

"Well, you could have fooled me. When you came for the job interview, I thought you were the most confident man on the planet and you bounded up these stairs, to pick me up for a date, with all the confidence of Genghis Khan racing into battle."

I kissed his cheek.

"Keep that up and we'll never get to dinner," he said, walking us to the curb.

He opened the door of a blue car, and said, "Be my guest, Princess."

When he got in, I asked, "Where's the Ferrari?"

"I've changed cars. This is a Porsche Taycan Turbo." He started the engine, took off smoothly, and headed towards the main street. "Do you like the color?"

"Love it. What's it called?"

"Gentian Blue Metallic. This car isn't really a turbo. I like that. It makes me think that maybe we aren't what people think we are. My working peers would be surprised if they knew I was happily spending time assembling an antique loom. That's not the image they have of me. What do you say to that?"

"Don't tell me you have this car because it isn't what its name says it is? If that's the case, I say that you're off your rocker and you don't know the value of money."

"Hold on. I have this car because it makes more sense than the Ferrari. It was built to be city driven and was adapted later for racing. I can hardly wait to hear what your dad thinks of it. Look how much more room I have for my feet and the extra space for Prince, back there."

"Where is Prince?"

"He's with Naslund, the dog-sitter."

"David!" I said. "I don't know about you."

"And what is it about me that you don't know?"

"How many men do I know who drive a Ferrari, pick me up for a date in a Porsche, go on about foot room and space for his dog? Does Prince approve of this date?" I asked. "And a dog-sitter? Who has ever heard of a dog-sitter? That's outlandish."

He picked up on my teasing by saying, "Fiza. I don't know about you."

"And what is it about me that you don't know?" I asked.

"How many ladies do I know that would call me a gentleman for taking the slops from above and walking in front on stairs, to catch her when she falls? Fiza, we agreed that this is a date. What gentleman would bring his dog on a date?"

"Who is winning this exchange?" I asked.

He kept his eyes on the road, but I knew he was grinning. In the beginning, I thought his grin was sarcastic, and it irritated me, but now, I realize he grins when he's happy or being playful, and I've come to savor it. He took my hand, and said, "Who we think we are changes over time. I'm no longer a Ferrari, speed-means-everything, man. I've come to appreciate the engineering excellence, the performance of a Porsche. It suits me better. That's what this change of cars is all about. You know, Princess, you and I have the strangest conversations. Are you aware of that? Are they strange to you?"

"I wouldn't label them strange," I said. "I think they are unique."

"Do you know what I find unique about you?" he asked.

"Of course, I do. I own Gertrude."

"No." he said. "Well, yes, it's partly that and your quick sense of humor. You make me laugh. But it's not that."

"Then what?"

"At the drop of a hat, you quote well-known people, you quote books. How many people would know Genghis Khan? You must read a lot."

"I love to read. The books on my shelf are not for decoration. How about you? Do you like to read?"

"In engineering at university, we were required to take a minor in arts. I wasn't interested in anything that was offered, so I put the courses, that would mesh with my already heavy agenda, in a hat. I drew philosophy. I didn't even know the meaning of the word. We were assigned a lot of reading. The more I read, the more I got interested. I became a voracious reader. During my army stints, I loaded up with bags of books. They were my great escape. But I'm not like you. At a drop of a hat, I can't quote

Kant. I admire that about you. You have me googling stuff constantly. Do you have a favourite book?"

"Dr. Zhivago," I said, without hesitation.

"Why so?" he asked.

"It's a classic love story. A beautiful love story. I read it every January. It's exhilarating, promising, and sad. That love could survive through the cruel atrocities of war gives me hope for humanity. It's how I like to start the New Year," I said. "Some sweat it out at the gym; I like to curl up with Zhivago."

"I haven't read the book, but I saw the movie," he said. "I liked the winter scenes at the frozen palace. I understand Zhivago's emotional longing when he looked through the patterns on the frosty window. And I will never forget the thousands of daffodils that came up in the spring. I thought they were foreshadowing a happy ending. Laura left, and he stayed behind. They never found each other again. That is not a happy ending. Why would she leave him?"

"Those were dangerous times. She had the safety of their unborn child to think about."

"If you'll allow, I'll sing *Lara's Theme* for you tonight," he said.

I had heard him sing with Dad when we went to the Karaoke Café as a family, and I thought how well they harmonized. I've heard him singing now and then at work and thought he was good. Now, he set me wondering and I asked, "Are you a professional singer?"

"You be the judge. My goodness," he said as he parked, "we must have been speeding. The time flew. Again, no ticket. You must be my lucky charm or maybe it's the blue car."

"Or maybe it's because I know all the men down at the station. I bribe them handsomely," I said.

"Make me jealous and I'll feed you inked squid."

Laughing, we held hands and went in. The place, decorated with antique pictures of Ornskoldsvik, was hopping. A man and woman, he wore a colorful sash and she a matching long scarf, were singing into mics in the center of the room. I didn't know the lyrics, but the music bounced the few people who danced around the singers. There didn't appear to be a dress code—jeans with a t-shirt, just-come-from-the-office, and party dresses danced past as we were shown to a small table for two. The waiter lit the decorative candle that was ringed with fresh flowers. Tables circled the periphery and were arranged to give a view of what was happening in the center.

Swedish meatballs were the night's specialty. Swedish meatballs can he ordered in most eateries in this town, but each chef adds his or her special twist. Different combinations of spices, thick or thin, dark or light sauce. My tastebuds imagined cumin, paprika, and coriander because this place's meatballs weren't over-powered with onions and garlic. They were delicious. I was busy sopping up the sauce with fresh hunks of rye bread, when David commented, "You seem to be enjoying those. How do they pair with the wine?"

"The Pinot Noir is so silky," I answered. I lifted my glass and said, "Skal."

He raised his and echoed, "Skal."

We finished our lattes, then David excused himself to talk to the man in charge of the karaoke center. When it was his turn, he took the mic, looked at me and sang Lara's Theme. His eyes saw right into my soul. His beautiful voice vibrated my heart. It felt like I had grown gossamer wings and would, at any moment, fly off into the ethers. When he finished, people stopped what they were doing and gave him a standing ovation. I flew to him, and we hugged. He released me, put his hands on my face and drew it to his. We kissed. The crowd went crazy, clapping and whistling. I stepped back and said, "Thank you, David. That was lovely."

Sparks shot from his twinkling eyes. He winked. "The song or the kiss?" He offered me his hand, and asked, "Shall we dance?"

On the dance floor, our bodies clung. We were in step, jiving to the rhythm of a Juke Box Classic by the Wanderers—*Do You Love Me.* He didn't speak, but he had the loudest eyes. They told me we were sharing a delightful terpsichorean enchantment. He twirled me away then back, ever closer and closer. Our impulses and desires surfaced and drifted away in a wave that washed over me in glorious elation. And it was obvious by how he looked at me and how close he drew me to him, that he also was caught up in the wild euphoria. A saying twirled in my mind, "How a couple dances is an indicator of how they'll be in bed." Rather than let it go, we allowed the mood to take hold. We caught the wave.

On the drive home, the mood continued. When he stopped the car, we hugged and kissed passionately. He abruptly broke away saying, "It's well past the witching hour. Let me see you safely upstairs before the ghosts come out."

I felt rejected but decided that what he meant was: it's awkward making love in bucket seats of a car.

At my door, I had a moment of timidity. It wasn't lost on me how I had frightened other lovers away, and I didn't want an encore. I took his hands; he trembled. The look in his eyes was unfathomable, deep, and mysterious. I wanted nothing more than to take him to my bed.

"Thank you, David. The evening was wonderful," I said.

"I must thank you, Fiza. You've brought things back to life in me that I thought were dead. You make me feel things I haven't felt in... well, ever. We must do this again sometime." He started down the stairs. At the landing, he waved. "See you tomorrow," he said, and off he went.

Scene Fourteen

Tomorrow

At Gertrude's Place, David and I slipped back into our work routine as if *the date* had never happened. We made strides with Gertrude, but our relationship became stranger by the day. He seldom spoke, but when he did, he wouldn't meet my eyes. He either kept his head down or looked away. It made me think of Macbeth's[2] famous words, *"Tomorrow and tomorrow and tomorrow,"* and their meaning—*life is meaningless, useless, and empty; and that every day just creeps by like every other day.*

"David, coffee is ready."

After some delay, he took a few sips, and, without looking my way, said, "I'm going to walk Prince. Prince, come."

When he walked away, I raised my voice and asked, "May I come too?" He didn't answer. I heard the outer door slam shut. *What's wrong? Out, out, brief candle!*[3] came to me. I knew something was seriously wrong. I sensed that it had something to do with the death and loss of too many people he had loved. I wanted to help him, but he was having none of that. He wasn't having anything to do with me. *Maybe, I'm the problem. Maybe, he's afraid to love me.*

---

[2] Macbeth (Act 5, Scene 5, lines 17–28)
[3] Macbeth (Act 5, Scene 5, lines 17–28)

He came back the next day, but his mood hadn't improved. The wooden checking block was rotten and I had ordered a new one. It had arrived, so we were putting it in place, a finicky job. The checking block prevents the pulling back stick from falling forward, which would make the shuttle *bang off.* The head of the bolt that came with the new part was too big. It inhibited the movement of the shuttle.

"Shit." David remarked, as he scrounged around looking for a bolt with a smaller head. When he put it in place it was too long and caught the picking leather whip. "Damn." Without a glance in my direction, he said, "Put in the ear plugs," and he sawed off the bolt. When he finished, he mouthed something, and I took out the plugs. "I need the ring of hex keys," he yelled.

"There's no need to yell. I've taken out the plugs." I wanted to add, *what happened to please and thank you*, but I didn't. That would be shoving salt in the already stinging wound.

He twisted the bolt with such force that the hex key bent. "These are shit." He voiced more foul invectives, threw the keys to the floor, and walked out.

Expletives being the order of the day, I called after him, "Shit, David, what's going on?" But of course, he didn't hear me. The door slammed. I was left alone with Shakespeare and his troubling words— "Double, double toil and trouble; Fire burn, and cauldron bubble."[4]

I sat on the floor and looked at the loom. *Have you come into my life to shape my destiny? Did you bring David? No wonder he won't accept a wage. This way he comes and goes as he pleases. Have I been at the beck and call of a troubled man? What price have I paid because I so desperately wanted my dreams for you to become reality?*

---

[4] Macbeth (Act 5, Scene 5, lines 17–28)

However, I wasn't without empathy for David. I knew he had a sad childhood and suffered from wartime traumas, but it confused me that he didn't talk about what was troubling him, because it was obvious that he was in a bad way. I intuited that he realized he was letting me in, and he was panicking. "David," I had asked, repeatedly, "can you tell me what's bothering you?"

"Another time," was always his come back, "can't you see that I'm busy." I sensed his body cringe.

When the hurly burley's done, I thought, *will he have lost his battle or won?*[5]

A month went by and David never came back. He didn't even send a message. I had to assume we had strutted our hour on the stage and it all signified nothing.

The girls at The Store sympathized with me. Even though, in the beginning, they hadn't been overly enthusiastic about the loom, they became encouraged as Gertrude shaped up. "You must accept that David is gone," Sue said. "Let me help you put an ad in the paper. We'll find someone else."

---

[5] A reference to Macbeth (Act 5, Scene 5, lines 17–28)

Scene Fifteen
Wool and Dyeing Conference

I had booked my flight to Ireland a few months ago, wanting to attend a wool and dyeing conference and to visit Grand Aunt Ellie and the gang. But David and I were getting to know each other. I wasn't sure that I wanted to be away from him for a couple of weeks and many times thought about cancelling. Sue had convinced me that David wasn't coming back. "He's unreliable," she said. "I couldn't understand why you put up with his comings and goings. You're better off without him."

"What choice did I have?" I asked. "As you remember, people weren't breaking down the door offering to help me with Gertrude. And besides, I intuited that there was an honest, nice person somewhere under all that gruff and unreliability."

"And you don't have a choice now. We're tired of all your moping," she said lightly. "You're going to Ireland, and I'm going to drive you to the airport to make sure you get on the plane."

I hugged her. "Thank you, Sue. I knew I could rely on your bossiness," I said.

"When you get back, I'll have a dozen people lined up for the job. Hone your intuition; you're going to need it. And your return date is on my calendar. I'll pick you up."

The evening before the conference, the organizers had a meet and greet gathering. The room had a buffet of finger foods. Stand-up-to tables, with white cloths and small floral centerpieces, were scattered strategically. "You had better snatch one of those shrimp canapés. They seem to be a favourite." The older woman in front of me suggested.

"Thank you, they look tempting. My name is Fiza," I said, pointing to my name tag, as people often had trouble with it. "I'm from Sweden," I added.

"Pleased to meet you, Fiza. I'm Eleanor. I'm from Estevan, Saskatchewan, Canada. Are you here alone?"

"Yes."

"Would you like to share a table? I'm here with my daughters and granddaughters. We have a family business. They're circulating. I can't walk and carry a drink and a plate. I would never get to eat anything, and I've spotted petit cream puffs up ahead. My favorites."

"That would be lovely, Eleanor. I too have juggling problems. And I would like to know why you have a red flower on your name tag. There are a few low tables with chairs. Follow me, I'll find us one."

When we were settled, she said. "I'll tell why the red flower tomorrow. There's a time slotted for participants to introduce themselves. What about you? Are you going to give us a show and tell?"

"I'm thinking about it," I answered.

"I'll look forward to it."

Having finished our refreshments, we stood, and she said, "Now, we must circulate."

"See you later, Eleanor. Enjoy yourself."

The next day, when I introduced myself, I spoke about my antique English shuttle loom and how I wished to weave heirloom blankets. "I not only want my blankets to be sustainable, but I wish them to have a soul, a sensitivity. I'm here to learn what wool would be best to use and where to source it."

A woman, about my age, wearing a hand knit, sky-blue sweater stood. "I'm Sophie from the US. I would suggest a superfine lambswool. I have some samples. I would be happy to show them to you."

"Thank you. I appreciate your help."

A handsome middle-aged man, greying at the temples, stood. I noticed his formal attire. *Smart dresser*. "I'm Gregory from England. My family has been in the textile business for three generations. May I suggest you use a mixture of threads. A pure wool blanket doesn't hold its shape very well."

"What do you recommend?" I asked.

"I suggest 70% wool and 30% cotton."

"Thank you. All this information really helps. I look forward to talking to you at your booth."

A young girl, with a long blond braid brought forward, stood. "I'm Heidi from Amsterdam. I think the cotton should be organically grown, ring-spun," she said. She fiddled with her braid as if she were nervous.

"Heidi, I like the idea of organically grown. I want my blankets to be eco-friendly, but I don't know what ring-spun is. Can you explain the term?"

She stopped fidgeting. "There's ring-spun and open-end spinning. Open-end is used in the high production textile industry. Ring-spun is an older, slower spinning method. It produces a stronger and softer yarn. I have samples. Come and test them. I think you'll feel the difference."

The introduction time was over. Eleanor must have spoken earlier. A short coffee break ensued. There were drink stands where you could get a variety of teas, help yourself to a coffee machine, or cold drinks—iced teas or juices in bottles. An array of pastries was spread out on a long table at the back of the room.

"Can I help you decide?" came a lovely, baritone, male voice from behind.

I jumped. For a flash, I thought of David and turned, "Oh. Hi Gregory."

"Sorry, I didn't mean to startle you."

"Do you mean help me decide on which wool to use or which pastry to eat?" I asked with a dollop of cheek.

"Both. But seeing as we are taking a break, the French macarons melt on your tongue."

"I think I'll try the shortbread cookies. The British really know how to make shortbread." The bell rang to announce that the next session would begin in five minutes.

"Next up is about dyeing," I said. "I'm clueless. I want to get up front. Talk to you later, I must run." I picked up some goodies and left.

"Later, then." He spoke to my back.

"There's no need to record my lecture; you can download it from my website," the dyeing presenter began. "If it helps, you can follow along using the pamphlets on your seats. To understand the dyeing process, we need to look at some basic chemistry. There are certain words we use that might be confusing. Their definitions are in the pamphlets."

"Instructions come with the dye packages. I just follow the steps in the right order," a woman said, standing. I wondered if she had been there on purpose to help direct the speaker.

"That's true. But creative people like to make their own dyes. They like to play around, experiment, try to get a desired color. For those people, a little basic knowledge is helpful. Color molecules bind to fabrics differently. Strength of dye and timing are also variants. I'll be making suggestions on what in nature produces good dyes." After that lecture, my head was spinning. I had learned a lot. I now realized that my heirloom blanket project with brand colors was going to take some time, but I was eager to start experimenting with dyes.

The afternoon was Booth Time. I found Gregory's and asked him to demonstrate his wools. "My products are dyed, ready to go," he said. "I thought you were going to dye your own, have a unique brand color."

"That's my down-the-road dream," I answered. "For now, I want to get Gertrude weaving." I gave him my loom's specifications.

"You'll want a strong, smooth, with little stretch thread for the warp. You don't want it to catch through the heddles and the reed. Your loom has a 15-dent reed. That means your cloth will have 15 warp strings per inch. That'll make a fine, lovely material. I suggest this tightly woven wool yarn," he said. You can choose the color and I'll see if I have matching weft yarns." I learned more about weaving from Gregory than from any of the lectures. In the end, I ordered enough yarn in soft rose and heather blue to produce twelve blankets, if I was going to incorporate the 30 % cotton threads. Next, I was off to find Heidi's booth. Again, I added a bundle to my weaving knowledge, mostly the unique jargon of weavers, and ordered a variety of colors to match the wool ones I had ordered.

"The order will arrive in two to three weeks," Heidi said. "I hope your blankets will be grand."

By that time, my head was swimming with colors, facts, and ideas. Who would blame me if I couldn't remember the address of The Store? I hoped I'd filled in the order forms correctly. I left Heidi and wandered about aimlessly. "Fiza," I heard a voice call. It was Eleanor. "Come in. Take a load off your feet. It's a bit crowded here at the booth, but I have a spare chair. Sit down. So nice to see you."

"Thank you, Eleanor. I'm exhausted." I put my bags down and sat. She introduced me to one of her daughters who took her turn at managing the family booth. "How's it going?" I asked Corrina.

"Busy," she answered. "People are as interested in the Red Lily as they are in our long mohair sweaters." She turned to her mother and said, "We should have brought more."

"And overweighted the plane."

"Your sweaters are lovely. I'd love to buy that periwinkle blue one. May I?" I asked.

"Of course. I'll wrap it for you."

"Thank you. Eleanor, I missed your introduction this morning. Can you tell me about the red flower?"

"I overslept and missed it. It must have been the jet lag, but people are asking here at the booth, so that makes me happy."

"And I'm asking."

"Well," she began, it's a western red lily. They were once very common in Saskatchewan."

"My mom was born in Canada, but I've never been. I've read that wild horses still roam there. That intrigues me."

"I haven't seen any, but I believe some still survive in the Cariboo region. The red lily, like the wild horses, is becoming an at-risk species. It used to grow in the wild, but urban sprawl and farming have affected its habitat."

"Why are you so interested in this flower? I thought you were a wool lady."

"The red lily is our province's floral emblem. In honor of Saskatchewan's 100th anniversary and because of the fear of it becoming extinct, a plant shop in town gave out 100,000 seedlings. Our shop caught the enthusiasm and every time someone purchased something, we gave them a seedling. It was the red lily that started our interest in plants. Our shop soon morphed into a wool and plant shop. It makes it more a year-round thing."

"You've given out many seedlings here at the conference. Why would you do that?"

"It's native to North America, but there are similar climates in other countries. It pleases me to think that not only has it survived but that its brilliant red petals will give many people pleasure. Besides, it's our signature calling card. People stop and ask about the flowering plant."

"You're an astute businesswoman. Do you have any seedlings left? You've given me an idea. Outside my shop window is sort of like being in the wild. It'll be the perfect spot."

"It needs sunny moist soil. It grows slowly and can be finicky. Do you have the patience?" she said, handing me a seedling.

"I can handle finicky," I remarked. "Thank you for the seedling and thank you Corrina for wrapping the sweater. Goodbye for now, I hope to meet you again sometime, Eleanor. Perchance, together, we might go see the wild horses."

After the conference, one of Grand Auntie's grandsons, who lives in Dublin, picked me up to drive out to the farm.

"Dia dhuit, my lovely Fiza," he said.

"Dia dhuit, my handsome Derek."

"Oh, my," he said, when he saw me laden with packages, "did you buy the store?"

"I did. I hope we're not riding your motorbike," I said.

"Life's a race," he said in a most lovely lilt. "I've brought my Super Sport Machine." It felt good to joke together. It didn't matter how long between visits, we cousins always picked up where we left off. There was an easy camaraderie with us.

When we were out of the city traffic, I said, "I love the limestone cliffs."

"It's July," Derek said. "I like them best in the fall when they have a bloom of moss and lichen."

"I spot some heathers and ambrosia. And I think I recognize rowan bushes."

"You would know for sure if it were fall. The rowans would be a blaze of red berries."

We drove past miles of pastures where contented sheep grazed. "The stone and hawthorn hedgerows are so unique," I said. "I haven't seen any in Sweden."

"They are an ecosystem onto themselves. Birds and all kinds of rodents live in them. This is 'hedgerow season.' No one can remove or even trim them when birds are nesting."

Before I knew it, we arrived at Grand Auntie's farm.

When we entered her house, there was a blast of excited greetings. "Hi everyone," I shouted over the noise, "I'm eager to catchup with you all, but first let me say hello to Grand Auntie."

"Of course," Derek said. Someone took my coat, and I was led into the parlor where Grand Auntie waited. I gave her a long gentle hug. "How very nice to see you," I said, close to her ear.

"Your hair smells good," she said. "Let me look at you. My, but you're looking perky. Now, sit here beside me. When the gang gets together there's a lot of noise, but we must find a moment. I want to hear all about the Ornskoldsvik folk. I'm a bit worried about Tree."

"Tree's fine," I said, "I'll tell you all the latest news, and I'm eager to share about the loom."

"And I'm eager to hear all you've to tell. You'll be staying in the guest house with two of the younger gals, but tomorrow on its stoop, we'll chat. The weather is supposed to be nice."

"That's so nice of you, Grand Auntie. You know how much it pleases me that you didn't have that original house torn down. You've made it into such a unique, lovely guest house. I like staying there. It has me imagining its history."[6]

"Well, tomorrow I'll share some of its stories, and perhaps you can tell me about your childhood in South Sudan. I know so little about that time of your life."

---

[6] Marlene F Cheng, A Mystical Embrace. Read about the Ireland home in this book.

I wasn't sure what I might share of myself. The thought of it made me uncomfortable. I would try to think of some happy stories. "Should I come and fetch you?" I asked.

"That won't be necessary. It'll take me some time, but I love being outside, and my feet have their imprints on that path. I'll be fine."

A little boy hopped past tinkling a tiny bell. "Thank you, Graham," she called after him, "we'll be right there." She said to me, "It's time to eat." I took her arm, and we went into the dining room. Two long tables had been set. I noticed polished antique silverware and the dinner plates were that Delft blue pattern with the birds and the curved bridge. *The Chinese have even influenced the Irish*, I thought, as I was directed to sit on Grand Auntie's right.

"It's your good side, isn't it Mom?" one of her sons asked. I assumed he was referring to her hearing. Her three sons had married and built their homes on this vast property. The daughters-in-law had volunteered to bring the food. They were advised to keep it simple. Large tureens were placed along the tables within reach of everyone.

When the lids were removed, the heavenly smell of Irish stew wafted towards me. "Oh my, how I've missed this," I added to the other oohs and ahhs.

"Pass the salads around," another son said, "I thought those two big wooden bowls full should do it. The ladies put me in charge. I picked the greens from my hothouse. The dressing is the family's well-kept secret, as you all know." He laughed.

"The Merlot is on the table," a grandson, who had taken charge of the drinks, said. "And those jugs have iced tea or lemonade. If anyone wants a pint, there's plenty in the cooler. Just whistle."

Everyone's mouth was busy either sharing catch-up stories or eating. When I sipped my wine, I savored the taste of plums, black cherries, and earl gray tea. I had a flash thought of David. *He would appreciate how well this wine paired with the stew.*

"This artisan bread is perfect," a granddaughter said. "It's got heft, and I love all these grains. Did you bake it in your outdoor oven?" she asked one of her aunts.

"Indeed, I did," the aunt answered, lifting her glass. "Cheers, Fiza. We're so glad you came."

An echo of cheers followed. I lifted my glass. "Cheers," I said, "I'm so happy to be here and to see you all. Thank you."

My two weeks away went by all too quickly, and before I knew it, I was on the plane home. Having spent time with my large extended family satisfied a deep longing in me. I felt refreshed. Content. I was ready to start life anew, without David.

Scene Sixteen

Airport Pick-Up

At the arrival gate, I glanced around for Sue. I thought I recognized another person. He leaned against a pillar at the end of the walkway, positioned so he couldn't be missed. I did a double take. My mouth opened in shock; my stomach flipped; it was David. *Oh God!* I thought. *How can I hide? He already sees me.* He came forward and took the handle of my suitcase. "My, you don't travel light. What's with all those packages?"

Should I retrieve my suitcase and say, thank you, but I'm meeting Sue? Or perhaps, I don't need your help, David. Sue is coming. But the words I managed to stutter were, "They're mostly samples."

"How was your trip?" he asked.

"Busy, I learned a lot. I want to set up a dyeing area and try some of the ideas."

"Fiza, Sue's not coming to pick you up," he said. "I volunteered because I need to talk to you. Can we go to the Tree Grove before I take you home?"

"That's fine. I'm in no hurry. It's been a few weeks since you walked out on me without an explanation," I said. "You left me high and dry. I know you weren't on the payroll, but that was your choice. I thought you had enough integrity to finish the job or to at least let me know that you didn't want to continue."

"That's what I want to talk to you about," he said.

We drove in his blue car, mainly commenting on trivial things such as the weather.

At the Tree Grove, he sat quietly for a few moments.

I assumed he was gathering his thoughts.

"I was trapped in guilt and fear," he said.

"Why, David?" I asked.

"When I vowed not to let anyone close, I promised my sister that for the rest of my life I would only love her. Whenever I looked at you, I had a guilt-driven panic attack. I was in love with you, and I didn't know how to handle it. And fear overtook me. I didn't know how it was going to happen, but I knew, like everyone else I had cared for, that I would lose you."

"Why didn't you talk to me about it?" I asked.

"Please, Fiza. Hear me out."

"I'm listening."

"With you, I thought I was becoming the man I wanted to be. I wasn't expecting this relapse. I knew I was slipping back, and it frightened me. My thoughts were haunting. Night terrors kept me awake. Food didn't interest me. I asked my sitter to take care of Prince, because I didn't have the energy to run."

"All the more reason why you should have told me. Did you think I wouldn't understand? Did you feel that I wouldn't care?"

"Fiza, I was scared. I wasn't thinking straight. The day I walked out, I had, at last, accepted that I needed help. I drove to the psychiatrist's office."

"And how did that go?" I asked.

"When I saw her, I couldn't stop talking and crying. I blubbered, on and on. She tried to talk me down. 'What are you feeling, David?' she asked, over and over. 'I think I'm suicidal,' I confessed. 'Do you wish to be admitted to the psychiatric ward at the hospital?' she asked. 'Please,' I said. She admitted me. An IV was started to balance my fluids and to administer sedatives. I slept for days, only waking to go to the bathroom or to try eating."

"I'm so glad you got help," I said.

"After that," he continued, "I had several sessions with the psychiatrist. She convinced me of what I already knew but couldn't convince myself to be true."

"And what was that?" I asked.

"The psychiatrist told me that I had to accept my sister's death, that she was gone. She said, 'If Elaine were here, she would be happy that her brother was in love. No sister would want her brother to feel guilty because he found someone to love.'"

"How do you feel about that, David?"

"I know that is true, but I had lived with my version of my promise to her, for so long, I needed help to get it out of my head. The psychiatrist helped me unpeel the bitter onion of my life and had me look at, and accept, through copious tears, every layer. With every tear, I was grieving all those that I had lost and hadn't let myself grieve. When I look at you now, my heart doesn't race in a guilty panic."

"David, I'm happy for you, but I don't understand why you didn't tell me what was going on. Why couldn't you talk to me?"

"I felt terrible that I was falling into a deep hole that I couldn't dig myself out of, and the deeper I fell the more difficult it became. I couldn't look at you, let alone talk to you. More than anything else, I wanted your respect. I'm so sorry that I've hurt you and damaged us. Is there any way that we can start over? Has too much happened?"

"How do I know that tomorrow you won't decide you can't love me."

"I can't promise you that won't happen, but I can tell you it is highly unlikely."

"What makes you say that?" I asked.

"The psychiatrist had me understand that in war, the chance of losing a mate is highly likely. She repeatedly stressed that what happened wasn't my fault. She told me that in civilian life my chances of losing someone I cared for was the same as everyone else's. She said that people don't stop living because they fear the future. They take risks every day. They fall in love, get married, and have kids. She asked me if I wanted to miss out on love and life because I'm afraid of the future. 'You're a bigger man than that, David,' she said. 'My advice to you is—jump off the high board.'"

"Did you understand what she was trying to tell you?" I asked.

"I took all that to heart, but I also put a safety net in place."

"How's that?"

"I've set up regular meetings with the psychiatrist, and I've promised her, if I feel a derailment coming that I would hightail it into her office, with or without an appointment. That's why I can say it's highly unlikely."

"David," I said, "I appreciate that you've been open with me. You and I can only work if we don't shut each other out. Let's promise never to stop talking."

"I'll do my best," he said, taking my hand.

I realized how much I had missed his touch. It was reassuring. A flood of warmth spread through me.

"I, also, will do my best," I said. "Let's take it slowly, day by day, and see what happens. What do you say to that?"

"I say that would make me very happy. Thank you, Fiza, for standing with me. Let me repeat; I will do my best."

"I don't feel secure when you flip in and out of my life. When one moment we're happy together and the next you run away, it keeps me on an emotional rollercoaster. But now that you've given me an explanation and we've promised to talk about what's happening to us, perhaps we can move forward more smoothly. I missed you, David."

"I can't tell you how much I've missed you. My heart ached to be back on that dance floor with you. I wanted so much to look into your eyes like I did that night and not feel guilty. Do you have plans for the rest of the day?"

"I've just landed, I haven't got that far," I said.

"Do you think we can pick up Prince and go for a walk on the beach? What do you say?"

"I say that would be lovely. I've also missed Prince."

I went with David to pick up his dog. Prince came running to me, pushing his head into my knees. He wanted me to ruffle him. "I don't think he's forgotten me," I said, feeling pleased. At the beach we threw sticks for Prince and ran and frolicked barefooted in the foam. I slipped, and David caught me. We held each other close, until we both began to cry. Our tears intermingled. We kissed them away.

"Fiza," he said, "I'm so sorry for what I've put you through. You can't imagine how much your understanding means to me. Thank you, from the bottom of my heart."

"Someday, David, I'll tell you my story. Perhaps it'll give you a better understanding of where my empathy has its roots."

"I would love that. It seems that everything has been all about me. Whenever you're ready. I'll be waiting."

On the short drive to my turret, we held hands. He drove slowly. *Is he stretching out the time*, I wondered. *Or has he changed his driving habits?*

"Do you need anything?" he asked. "A few groceries?"

"Thank you, but I'll be fine. I put some milk and bread in the freezer."

"Can you freeze milk?"

"As long as you give it room to expand."

He carried my suitcase upstairs, retrieved the key, and let me in. "I'll leave you be, for now," he said, and gave me a gentle hug. "Call if you need anything."

When I closed the door, I twirled around the room. "Hello turret," I sang. "I'm happy to be home." I stripped down, took a warm shower. In lounging pajamas, I felt refreshed, and started to unpack. When I opened the package from Eleanor's booth, I got a surprise. There was a pale, rusty-reddish sweater. *Hmm, that's odd. I distinctly remember asking for the periwinkle blue.* I cuddled its softness to my face and went to have a look in the mirror. *This color's perfect. I love it.*

Scene Seventeen

David Comes for Dinner

David and I planted the red lily seedling where we could see it from the window in the kitchen of Gertrude's Place. "You say it's finicky. I'll help you nurture it," he said, patting the earth. "We should set up a watering schedule."

"I can imagine it flourishing." I spread my arms wide. "It's a slow grower but someday, I can see a large red cluster here. Perhaps I'll hand out seedlings to our customers."

"I've never met anyone with such a gigantic imagination," he smiled, gathering the gardening tools.

"Joyce Kilmer's words come to mind," I said. "I think that I shall never see, a poem as lovely, as a tree."

"Did you say Joyce Kilmer?" he asked. "Is she Canadian?"

"Yes. Why?"

"A Canadian soldier nailed a prayer on the wall of the barracks in Afghanistan. If I recall correctly, the author was Joyce Kilmer."

"Do you remember any of her words?"

"My rifle hand is stiff and numb," he said. "That's about it."

"Interesting," I said. "It's words that we can relate to that stick."

"You must relate to a lot of things. Words are stuck all over you." He grinned.

"Ooof," I said, raising an eyebrow. "I think that's a compliment."

"I like the way I can talk about my time in the service without getting hit with an uninvited panic rush," he commented.

"I'm happy for you, David." I hooked my arm through his and gave it a squeeze as we walked into Gertrude's place. "Loom builders. Gardeners. Human beings, extraordinaire!"

"And we must get started on the dyeing room," he said.

"Loom builders. Gardeners. Dye room experts. Are there any more specialties you would like me to add?"

He winked and said, "I'll think about it."

We became Ikea rats, and from our sleuthing started to build a dyeing room in Gertrude's Place. I hired an electrician and a plumber, but David and I did all the construction. We were now experts at putting together Ikea shelves and cabinets. "As a team," David said, "we should put ourselves out for hire."

I arched a single eyebrow—my favorite skeptical look.

"I've enjoyed planning this space with you," he said. "Putting Gertie aside, for a while, and concentrating on something new feels good."

"I agree. It's as if we're designing and executing a new way of being together."

"And I think we're set on a firmer foundation," he answered.

"I like the way you look at me when you speak," I said, "even stopping what you're doing."

"These eyes can't get enough of you."

"Let's hang this plaque that I bought at the conference," I said, wanting to divert the conversation. My feelings for David were starting to get intense and they frightened me, for some reason I didn't quite understand.

"You and plaques," he said, feigning exasperation. "**There's magic in what the dye gods give you on any given day,**" he read. "I like that. You'll be able to start your magic any time now."

"To celebrate our accomplishments, would you like to come to dinner at the turret?" I asked.

"Thank you, Fiza. I would love that. When?"

"Tomorrow evening. Does that suit you?" *What have I done? How is this going to tamper the intensity of my feelings?*

I fretted the entire time I was preparing dinner for David. *I should have stuck to something simple. A savory cheese soufflé for heaven's sake; it's*

the most difficult dish to perfect. Mine is certainly not 'as light as air.'
Perchance its 'full of flavor' will impress him. Why was I trying to impress
him. I heard David's footsteps bounding up the outside stairs. I patted
down my hair, wiped the worry look from my face, and went to greet
him. He dashed in, slipped out of his loafers, and held out an over-sized
bouquet of red camellias. "Sparks flying," he said.

"Sparks flying? What do you mean?" I asked, accepting the flowers.
"Red camellias represent a flame in my heart. My interpretation is
'sparks flying.' Don't you think it's apt?"

"I think you are sentimental but shy to let me see it. Thank you, they
are lovely." I kissed his cheek.

"Oh my, that certainly was nice. Give them back. I'll make another
entrance if I get one of those on the other cheek," he said.

"You're a tease," I said. "Come in. Help me cut their stems and find
a big enough vase." After our flower arranging, he took the bouquet in
its Delft Blue vase and set it on the windowsill. I stood back to look.
"Beautiful," I said.

"We've broken off a flower. Do you have a dish to float it in?" he
asked. He placed the vintage dish with the floating flower on the short-
legged table, among the cushions on the floor, where we would dine. We
sat.

"I've made us a cocktail," I said, offering him a glass.

"Skal," he offered, lifting his glass to me. "This is romantic."

"Skal." I clinked his glass. "Are you comfortable?"

"Very."

"Me, too."

"Wherever did you get that twisted candle? It looks like a curvy, sexy
woman."

I laughed. "Somewhere in de Wallen, a red-light district in
Amsterdam. Lex Pott is the designer, I believe."

"Have you travelled a lot?" he asked.

"Some. Travelling is like walking through sand. It's impossible not to
leave your mark. I think it's sad how tourism can change a place. I shirk
the Taj Mahals and the Eiffel Towers of the world. I like the alleys, the
marketplaces, the surprise of coming upon a lesser known cathedral. The

people. As reminders of a place, I prefer sleuthing out interesting objects that speak to me. I don't want to have just gone a very long way. I want the magic of a place to transform me."

"I like your free-wheeling approach to life and to your one-of-a-kind eating place. In a formal setting, I'm confused. I feel uncomfortable. I don't know which fork to use."

"I never grew up with rules on how to set a table, so I've taken free rein. Frivolity and mood are my guides. I challenge myself to speak to my guest's innate spirit."

"I like that. What is my innate spirit? May I ask?"

"I'm getting to know your self-expression," I said.

"Oh?"

"It's changed."

"How so?"

"That first day when you came to The Store you were so macho. You had such a confident air that said you knew exactly who you were, and you were unapologetic about it. I wanted nothing to do with such a pompous ass and was determined to dismiss you. But somehow, I intuited something else. I became curious as to what was hiding underneath such a brazen exterior. Besides, you appeared to know how to put Gertrude together. How could I let you go?"

"Wow! You don't pull any punches," he said. "Am I still that pompous ass?"

"Only at times." I winked at him, smiling. "No, David, you are not. You're humble and caring."

He took my hand. "Thank you, Fiza. That means a lot to me."

Let's have dinner," I said.

"This is the best soufflé I have ever tasted. Yummy. It has so much flavor. Are you up to sharing the recipe, or is it a family secret?" David pronounced while helping himself to seconds and thirds.

"Thank you, David. I found the recipe online. I was terrified that it might end up a floppy mess."

"A floppy mess? It's elegantly royal. Most soufflés take a nosedive. Yours stands proud."

After we finished eating, he helped me take the dishes into the kitchen. "I'll make coffee," I said.

"Please sit. Let me make the coffee," he insisted.

I went to the bathroom to freshen up. *He's become considerate. I can tell that he wants to know about me. He's not faking it. He's truly interested. When he gives me an opening, why do I panic and clam* up?

When I returned to the kitchen, he was measuring the coffee. To him it was an exact science. I leaned into his back and put my arms around him. *It feels good to be close to him.* He turned. I smoothed his hair back from his eyes. *He's letting it grow out a little.*

"Do that," he said, "and you won't get coffee any time soon."

I kissed his lips.

"Thank you for tidying up. If I'm ever looking for a house-helper, I'll put up another Starbucks' ad," I said.

When we settled back on the cushions, he asked, "What is it, Fiza, that you want from life? What are your dreams?"

Here it is. Another opening. It felt a little too personal. Perspiration gathered between my breasts. I felt a rush of red start up my neck and flush over my face.

"I'm happy with my life. I'm happy where I'm at. I can't wait to have Gertrude weaving."

"You mean when or if we get her to work. That must be a future dream."

"I have full confidence in you. There's no doubt in my mind you'll have her working, soon."

"Is that it?"

"I want The Store to shift gears, somewhat. I dream of adding beautiful, wool-woven heirloom blankets to the inventory. The store needs to be more than cotton textiles."

"Have you thought about where the wool will come from? Don't tell me I'm going to become a sheep farmer!"

"Or a raiser of alpaca or yak. And when I get this art of dyeing down to a science, I'll develop one of a kind colours unique to The Store. But..." I paused to think of the right words. I didn't want to sound like I was coming on to him.

"But?" he asked, imitating my one raised eyebrow look. "Don't you have dreams for the future beyond Gertie?" he persisted.

"Yes, I do. I dream of loving a man who loves me. I want to be married. A house with a big backyard where our apple tree drops fruit on both sides of the fence, where all children are welcome to play. A meeting place for neighbours and friends."

"But haven't you found that Swedish people like to keep to themselves? Not that they are snobbish, necessarily. It seems to be in their nature".

"You're right. Most often, they take their time opening to strangers, but once they get to know you, they can be delightful."

"You're probably right. I don't have many Swedish friends but the few I have are fiercely loyal and a lot of fun. Skal," he said, lifting his cup. "Here's to your dreams. They sound lovely. I saw moonbeams in your eyes."

"Thank you, David. Tell me, do you dream?"

He hesitated, fiddled with his watch, then said, "My dreams have centered on a big pay cheque, a fancy car, Gucci loafers..."

"Oh?"

"When I was on the skids, I decided to reconstruct myself. I had a fixed image of the person I would be. You know all those things I just mentioned."

"And you have accomplished all that."

"I fell prey to those tiger goals. I ignored every paw scratch warning and look where it got me. I ended up an unglamorous mess. My relapse showed me that no matter how hard I had been paddling, I was stuck in murky shallow waters. In that miasma, I knew I was hiding from what happened. Once more, I had to take a serious look at *me*. I asked myself, *is all this enough?*"

"And how did you answer?"

"No."

"What was missing?" I asked.

"Love."

I reached over and touched his arm.

"All my life I've hungered for love. To be loved and to love. To feel what love feels like. And as you already know, after my experiences, I was scared to death to let anyone close. I knew that the pain of losing another person would finish me."

I moved closer and put my arms around him.

"My next question was, *who am I?*" he said.

"Could you find an answer to that?"

"What came to me was the opposite to the image I had been fixated on. Fiza, I've come to believe I'm a bigger person than that pompous ass. Wasn't that how you described me?"

"Where does one begin to figure out who they really are?" I asked, giving him a cuddle. I felt him relax. My tension dissipated. This cuddle seemed special. *I think this is a special moment. A moment we can build on, for us.*

"I hadn't a clue. I just knew I had to give up all that pretense. I started asking myself, *what makes me happy? What makes me truly happy?*"

"Have you figured that out?" I asked.

"First off, when I'm down-and-out dirty trying to put Gertie together, I'm content. She challenges me. She gives me satisfaction. There is nothing else I would rather be doing."

"I see that, David. Your concentration amazes me. The whole atmosphere of you at work is daunting. An earthquake couldn't shake you."

"Secondly, when I'm caring for Prince, I feel responsible. He depends on me, and I wouldn't have it any other way. I cherish our companionship."

"I know," I said, kissing him on the cheek. "I don't mind playing second fiddle to Prince."

He gave me a squeeze. "Interesting that you said *fiddle.* I was thinking about how to tell you about something else that stirs me."

He stirs me. I want, so much, for him to hold me close. "How on earth could fiddle fit into this conversation?" I asked, trying to keep my emotions in check.

"Have I told you the guitar story?"

"Not that I recall, but I wouldn't be averse to hearing it. Let's make more coffee. You can tell me the guitar story but that doesn't let you off the hook. I still want to hear all the things that make you happy."

"I saw dishes of chocolate mousse on the kitchen counter. Have we forgotten about dessert?" he asked. He grinned like a small boy who had been caught with his hand in the cookie jar.

"I haven't forgotten," I said. "Do you want dessert before or after your story?"

"I think better with a treat."

I appreciated that David showed me respect and hadn't pushed to hear my story. I wasn't ready. In the meantime, he shared more of himself and our relationship bloomed. *When the opportunity arises and I'm ready, I will tell him. I have a feeling it might be soon.*

Scene Eighteen
The Guitar Story

"When I was in senior high," he said, "I played the guitar in a school band. It was an Epiphone ES335 Casino—electric.[7] A semi-acoustic, actually, because of its full hollow body. When I practiced in the music room—which was every spare moment I could squeeze out—even with the guitar unplugged, I attracted an audience. The teachers encouraged this. The school had problems getting some students interested in anything, and they must have noticed some of the more difficult to discipline ones hanging out with me and had deemed that a positive."

"Is that Casino a good guitar?" I asked.

"Ask the Beatles. They made it famous. It has tonal flexibility. It was fun trying to imitate the sounds that the Beatles could coax out of their guitars. I especially liked Paul McCartney's creativity, after the group had disbanded. It's a songwriter's guitar."

"Wow! The Beatles!"

"The school band played at school dances and some assemblies. Because the Casino is lightweight, it is easily portable. Four of us formed a group—The Yellowjackets—and we did gigs around town to earn a few bucks. My happiest days during those school years were all associated with music. When I graduated, I was given the biggest surprise of my life."

"What was that?" I asked, feeling his excitement.

---

[7] All information about guitars came from a friend, Bob Orr, a guitar aficionado. He lives on Vancouver Island, B.C., Canada

"The music teacher presented me with a guitar. It was an Epiphone DR100. An acoustic. He said, 'No one else will make this guitar sing like you can. It is my pleasure to present it to you in gratitude for all the pleasure you have given us. Thank you, David. You will be missed.'"

"Oh my, how wonderful," I said. "You must have been one cool dude."

"The first time I played it, I noticed a plaque glued on the back of the guitar."

"What did it say?"

"To David Jones in appreciation of his dedicated excellence in music. Yellowjacket High. Starkville, Mississippi." After a minute or so, he added, "That guitar was the holy grail of my life. Probably because she was always strapped to my back, I named her Walker. At university, whenever I got a chance I played in a square or hallway. Students passing by threw coins into the case or gathered. Those coins treated me at Starbucks or to an occasional meal off campus. Walker saved my sanity on deployments. On duty, over and over, I repeated Bruce Cockburn's line, "Gotta kick at the darkness 'till it bleeds daylight."

"Did you get many chances to play when you were in Afghanistan?" I asked.

He didn't seem to hear me, and continued, "It was in the barracks the day of the accident. I never did find out what kind soul packed up my things, but I got them at the Walter Reed."

"Walker?"

"Yes, Walker. "

"I haven't seen it. I haven't heard you play. David, I would love to hear you play," I said.

"Walker ended up in a pawn shop in Washington," he said. "A guitar strumming, long-haired, Jimi Hendrix look alike didn't jive with the spiffy looking image I was determined to display. Besides, I needed the money.

"Oh, no." I gasped.

He ignored my reaction and said, "But with my latest look at *me*, I've acknowledged that without music, without a guitar, part of the real me is missing. I've been haunting every music store in town. Probably tried a hundred different guitars. Haven't found the right sound, yet."

He grinned.

"What's so amusing?"

"It just struck me," he answered.

"What just struck you?"

"I've probably been looking in all the wrong places."

"How so?"

"Perhaps I should be visiting pawn shops. Wouldn't that be ironic?" He paused, scratching at his chin. "Wouldn't that be ironic?" he repeated.

"Wouldn't it just," I answered him.

"And there's something else that would make me happy," he said.

"What's that, David?"

His eyes softened. His voice went nearly still. "I want to keep my future free and open. Let it unfold naturally. But I would like to have children," he said. I leaned closer. I didn't think I would ever hear those words from him. I felt all mushy in the stomach. "The thought doesn't frighten me anymore, but I haven't gotten as far as apple trees dropping fruit on both sides of the fence." His mischievous twinkle lit up his face. "I would plant honeysuckle bushes and there would be a minivan in the driveway."

I hugged him tight. "I'm so happy for you."

"Have you ever smelled honeysuckle aroma in the hot summer air?" he asked.

"I can't say that I have."

"Then, you haven't lived."

"Then, I would have to say that I'm ready. I jumped up and threw my arms in the air. "I'm ready to live," I shouted.

"Don't move away from me, Fiza. Come back. I want to tell you something." I sat beside him. "You've been my life changer. You've been more than what the doctor ordered. Because I was so focused on my fixed image, I almost lost you. And no one else has the foggiest idea who I really am."

This is the moment you've been waiting for, I told myself. *Act now.*

"Would you accept a gift in celebration?" I asked, walking to the bookshelf. My knees knocked at each other. *Am I about to jump off the high board?* I had a crystal that was known to help people who had had a mental breakdown. I wanted David to wear it, but I didn't want him to think I was interfering in his attempt to be well.

"Oh my," he said. "I'm not in the habit of receiving gifts from young ladies, but..."

"But what?"

"But I'm eager to see what you wish to gift me."

I opened my palm and showed him the heart-shaped lapis lazuli crystal. I saw a face I had never seen before. It told me that I had touched him deeply.

His eyes shone wet. "It's beautiful," he whispered.

I bent down and clipped it on his gold neck chain. "With love," I said.

He stood up and took me in his arms. "Thank you, Fiza. I'll cherish it." He kissed me and we clung together for a few moments, then he stepped back and said, "You and I need a break. We need some time alone together to figure out where we are going." I could tell this wasn't a spur-of-the-moment thing. He had probably been thinking about it, and without taking a breath or allowing for my reaction, he continued, "I know the perfect place to take a quick vacation. Have you been to the Islands?"

"Do you mean the archipelago?"

"Yes, did you know there are 30,000 islands? It's less than an hour's boat trip from Stockholm."

"Yes, I know about them. No, I have not been there."

"The minute you step off the boat, the pace drops. You go into island mode where time is different. It's just what we need."

"Oh." My mind was already racing ahead. A slight flush worked its way up my neck. *What will a few days alone together bring?* "When do you think we should go?" I asked.

"I think the sooner the better. Would this weekend suit you?"

"That would be fine. Do we have to book the ferry? What about hotel reservations?"

"I'll take care of all that. I'll be busy at the office for the rest of the week, but I'll let you know what time I'll pick you up on Saturday morning. Is that okay?"

"That's great. What a good idea. I'm looking forward to it."

"I must run," he said. He kissed me and added, "Pack light. We must walk on the ferry. See you on Saturday, probably early."

He left. At the landing, he turned back and waved. Nervous excitement brought out my cheek. I raised my voice and said, "In Canada, I've been told wild horses still roam. Perhaps we should go to Canada."

"For a weekend? I don't think so, love. Maybe another time. Hold it in your dreams."

Scene Nineteen

The floating structures, some bigger than others but all a newly painted, bright hue, vied for every inch of mooring. The berthing fenders were hard pressed to keep them from rubbing the quay or banging each other.

The occupants, kids, adults, even the elderly, toys, or mugs in hand, leapt back and forth between the vessels, conversing loudly over the splashing water, laughing, seemingly intoxicated on the sea air.

The land buildings, also of a fresh paint look, as in a child's story book, cuddled each other, leaving barely a few feet for a path to wander among them.

"We'll get lost in this maze," I said, feeling giddy with anticipation. "Did you bring rose petals?"

"Do you smell that?" David asked.

"It smells sweet or spicy, but I can't put a handle on it," I answered.

"It's cardamon. It's coming from that lean-to over there. Let's check it out."

"We've just had a savory scone. You can't be hungry already?" I teased him with my one-raised-eyebrow look.

That's what the Islands are all about," he countered, taking my hand, and steering us in the direction of the wafting scent. "A tasting tour."

We sat alfresco at a small wooden table that looked hand hewn. The waiter, dressed like a gardener with a white apron, set small cardamon buns on our table. "Fresh from the oven," he claimed. "I'm Olie. Are you visiting?"

Yes," I said, "we're from Ornskoldsvik. We just arrived this morning; we're enjoying your island."

"Olie, do you make lattes?" David asked.

"The best."

"You said earlier, Fiza, that you craved a latte. Is that what you would like?"

"Yummm."

"Two grand lattes please, Olie."

David gobbled up two of the small buns and sat back enjoying his coffee.

The buns were delicious. For me they demanded a slow take. Making them last, I lifted my face to catch some rays between bites and sips of the latte. I felt content, dreamy even. David broke my reverie by saying, "I think we were born for each other."

"Why do you say that, David?" I asked.

"I've shown you all of me, every wart, every wrinkle, and yet you are still here," he answered. "You've helped me let go of my fears. I can't imagine not letting you be close. Are you willing to take a chance on us?"

I wondered if this was a proposal and said, "I've been taking a chance on us for a long time. Why would I stop now?"

"Let's go to our room. Do you think the neighbours will mind if we go skinny dipping?" He winked.

"That might be fun, but the water is probably freezing."

"I doubt that," he said. "It's the beginning of August. Have you forgotten our April swim?"

"How can I forget? It was the first time that I had swam in the ocean, and I loved it."

Well, if you're not up for that, we can open that Rondo the management graciously left for us. I'll light the set-wood in the fireplace."

"That sounds more inviting. Do you think we can find our way back through the maze of wandering paths?"

"No problem. There's only one inn. I'll ask the friendly people if we are on the path to the Sea Gull. We'll be pointed in the right direction, besides, as you suggested, I dropped rose petals."

When he was busy lighting the fire, bellowing air to encourage the flame, I took the cushions from the sofa and placed them on the floor. I sat down and leaned against the sofa. *He's like the warmth of a fire when I'm cold. I wonder how close I can get before I get burned.*

He opened the wine and poured it into the glasses on the coffee table. He handed me a glass and sat down. "Skal," we toasted each other.

We sipped our wine, savouring its subtle sweetness, enjoying the warmth from the fire and each other. We shared soft kisses and caresses added to the heat.

"You're such a special person, Fiza," he said. "I'm happy being in love with you."

"I'm happy, too, David. This is blissful."

He stood and set our glasses on the table. He took my hands and brought me to my feet. "Come," he whispered, leading me to the bedroom. "I need to be closer to you."

We undressed each other and clinging, in a desperate attempt to get closer, we laid on the bed. I could taste the sweetness of wine on his tongue, and I wanted the entire cask of him. Our kisses weren't firefly flicks. They were deep, filled with passion, speaking our desires. They stole my breath away. His lips left soft imprints on my breasts, over my belly. I was drowning. Had we gone skinny dipping, after all? We were most certainly naked. We memorized the lines of each other, as if reading a love poem in braille, knowing where pressure was needed and softness was best. My insides had the warmth of scorching wild bushes. Sparks of longing shot from his deep penetrating eyes, like a meteorite filled sky. Moans of pleasure floated over me in waves.

Suddenly, my whole body cringed. I panicked, came undone, couldn't breathe.

"My God! Fiza. What happened? Have I hurt you? I didn't mean to hurt you." He tried to hold me.

"Don't touch me," I said, pulling away. Clenching my knees to my chest, I rocked and burst into tears.

Lines of confusion tightened David's face that had turned ashen. His eyes were filled with pain. Finally, I was able to reach out to him. He took me in his arms. I've never felt such tenderness. The flood gates re-opened and my tears wet his bare chest. He pulled a blanket over us, wrapping it tight around me, and continued to hold me close. I don't know how long we lay like that. He altered between wiping away my tears and stroking my body like a parent would to calm a child. I felt better and sat up. "Can you bring me a warm cloth, please?" I asked. He put on a robe and went to get the cloth. He sponged my face and brought a dry blanket for me to wrap in.

"I see this place has a machine. Can I make you a coffee?" he asked.

"Thank you, David. I need one."

We sat up on the bed leaning against the headboard, drinking our coffee. "Your tears taste of some truth you haven't shared with me," he said. "You've let me share my pain. Now, it's time for you to tell me yours. Don't rush, Fiza. I can wait. I'll sit here for the rest of my life if that's the time you need. I'm not going anywhere."

"When you first came into my life," I started, "you were abrupt, sarcastic. I thought you were undoing me to make yourself feel more put together, but I intuited that you were hiding something and that underneath your bravado you were a good person, and I stuck with you. And I'm glad I did. Tonight makes me realize just how wonderful a person you are."

"Fiza, you are doing it again."

"What am I doing, again?'

"Every time I try to get you to talk about yourself, you find a way to turn the conversation back so it's about me. This time, it isn't going to work. You came undone, and I'm here to help put you back together. Like I said, I'm waiting."

"What is there to tell? You know I have everything: a loving family, a career that I'm happy with, a man who I love and who loves me." I couldn't think of what else to say, so I took a drink of coffee.

"And yet?" he asked.

"And yet, David, I feel empty."

"And why do you suppose that is?"

"I don't know. I think it's because something is missing."

"What do you think is missing?"

"I don't know. There's something hidden in my memory that triggers my heart to panic. When my heart panics, I feel dirty, unworthy, not good enough."

"God, Fiza! I don't want you to ever feel like that. You are the most beautiful person I've ever met. Capable. Giving. Compassionate. Just look what you've done for me, drawing me out, allowing me to feel again."

"But David, I'm afraid. I don't want to know the bad parts of my past. What if they are horrific? I don't think I could handle that."

"What times in your life can't you remember?" he asked.

"I don't have any memory of my early teenage years. I know I've blocked them out. I've lived, hoping to keep them hidden in a place that I could never get at, but I'm beginning to realize I must find those lost parts of me. Maybe they'll fill my emptiness. "

My God, I thought. *What am I saying? Why am I talking to David about these things? I don't want my past to suddenly blow up and destroy my happy life. I could lose David. I must find a way to change the subject.*

"I know so little about your past, Fiza, and what I do know mostly came from your parents. I would like to hear your past, from you. I'm here for support if it's emotionally difficult for you."

"David, I would like another cup of coffee. Can you please make coffee? I need a shower."

"Fiza don't rush. Have a shower. I'll go for a quick run. When I come back I'll put the coffee pot on."

"Don't forget your headband light; it's dark out there."

Scene Twenty
Fiza's Story

After a shower and wearing the cozy housecoat the room provided, I felt refreshed, and settled on the cushions by the sofa. "Are you warm enough?" David asked.

"I wasn't rejecting you," I said.

"Fiza, I believe that. Not for a moment will I think that you do not love me, that you do not want me. You love me like I've never known love, and because of your love and understanding, I've let myself love you. I love you, Fiza, with all my being. That's why we must figure out what happened. You know everything about me. Now, it's time for you to tell me about you. Can you tell me?"

"I'm told that I was born early in the day, during the monsoons in Sudan. It was the time of the longest civil war in Africa's history—the Islamic North against the Christian South. I don't remember the euphoria that engulfed my people when the war ended, and my country, South Sudan, became the youngest country in the world thanks to the UN.

"However, the divorce wasn't neat and tidy; the border between Sudan and South Sudan was never marked decisively, and there were never-ending border skirmishes.

"But that wasn't the worst of it. Only a few years into South Sudan's independence, it had its own civil war. Ancient grudges that forgot how to heal, reared their ugly heads. Tribal uprisings, terroristic rampages, lootings and burnings, rapes, castrations, massacres. Hatred was everywhere, like barbed wire. There was no where to run without getting lacerated.

"My village was raided. I was kidnapped and taken to a terrorist camp. I was about ten years old.

"I only have flicking memories of that camp. But I do remember escaping. Thrashing in the bushes, trying to find the path back to my village.

"My aunt had got word that I was coming. She found me and took me to her tukul. With care, she washed my cuts and soothed my broken spirit. I can still feel her arms rocking me, still hear her voice encouraging me, 'Everything is all right now, Fiza. You are safe, love. Forget all that. Your nightmares must stop. You are safe.'

"When I had recovered strength, I asked to go to my mother and father. I needed to see them and my siblings. I had carried pictures of them in my mind ever since I was kidnapped. My determination to see them is what kept me hanging on when I was in the camp.

"My aunt held me tight and with tears running down her face, she told me the truth."

I couldn't go on. Tears came. I couldn't breathe. I lost control and thrashed at David, fiercely pounding his chest. "No. No. No." I hollered as my fists beat upon him.

"Fiza," David said, crushing me into him, blocking my fists, "everything is alright. You're here with me. I'm not letting go. You're safe. Fiza, you're safe. Fiza, this is David. I love you. I love you so much, Fiza. You are safe."

I sat back and blew my nose. "Please David, I need another warm cloth." When he came back, I said, "I'm sorry."

"There's never a need to say sorry between us. You're remembering painful things. Why shouldn't you cry?"

"Thank you. I thought I had hidden those things and that I would never have to remember. What is it about you, David? You have those memories coming back to me. It's almost like they happened yesterday."

I felt the warmth of the sun on my face and looked to the window. "My gosh, David," I said. "It's morning."

"Are you trying to divert our talk away from you?" he asked. "If it hurts too much, you don't have to tell me."

"No, David, I must tell you. This remembering is good for me. If I don't speak now, I doubt I ever will. Please let me tell you."

"Alright. Be gentle on yourself. What truth did your aunt tell you?"

'Your family is dead. The night our village was raided—that night of horror, raping, and burning—they murdered your family. Your family is dead. I'm sorry, Fiza. I'm so very sorry.'

He took my hand. I read fear in his eyes, but he said nothing.

"Of course, I couldn't believe her words. After all, my family had been with me the whole time I was away. 'How is little sister?' I asked her. 'I bet she's grown like a weed. Is little brother taking classes, yet?'

'Fiza, listen to me,' she said. 'They are all dead.'

'Father?'

'Yes, and your mother, and all the little children.'

'Where are they?'

'In the village graveyard.'

'What about my father's tukul? What about the tree he planted to give it shade?'

'They burned his tukul. The tree survived, but I don't know how it is. When you are ready, we can go look.'

"My mind couldn't reconcile with reality," I told David. "Reality was raw, visceral, and haunting. I was in a lost land, stumbling around in the bushes during the day, unable to eat the nourishing foods my aunt made special for me, screaming with excruciating nightmares, thinking of ways to kill myself.

"My aunt soothed me with her words saying, 'Please don't feel orphaned and alone. You are part of my family. You are wanted. Let me help you. Don't let anyone say you are useless. Gossip says that you are used goods. You are not. You are priceless. You will inspire every young girl in this village. The pain of loosing my brother, your father, and his family opened me up. I've never mended. And I worried every day about you. I knew you had been taken. I prayed for God to bring you safely back. And now, you are here. Together, we will find a way to live.'

"I'm surprised how I'm remembering my aunt's words," I said. "Why should I want to forget such a wonderful aunt?"

"That's good, but what you suffered is terrible," David said. "I understand how hard that is to share."

"I might have told you sooner," I said. "I know you gave me many openings to talk about myself, but as I've explained, I wasn't ready. Besides, your issues were important to me. I didn't want mine to get in the way."

"My sweet darling Fiza, we are cut from the same cloth. Don't you see the pattern here?"

"I do. Do you think you and I are going to work out?"

"Believe it!" he said.

"Do you think there's a way to mend our ragged cloth pieces? To stich us together?"

"I most certainly do."

"Thank you, David, for standing with me."

"Do you believe I love you?" he asked.

"Yes."

"And do you believe that you love me?"

"Yes, I know I do, with all my heart. With this croaky voice I may not sound convincing, but I'm sincere. The adventure of us gives me an immense feeling of belonging. I take that to be love. I'm starving. Can we go eat?"

"Yes, but I still want to know how you got from being suicidal to ending up in Sweden," he said. "But let's eat. This place boasts having the best Belgium waffles in all of Scandinavia. Let's see if it's true."

David had said it was supposed to be chilly today, so I was glad I had brought slacks and my warm, long, rusty-red mohair sweater. David changed from his jogging suit. He dressed in different shades of khaki and added a matching vest. Walking to the dining area, I was almost back to feeling like a tourist.

The waffles, all dripping with butter and dollops of blueberry jam, were better than advertised. When we lingered over coffee, David said, "I want to take something home for Prince. Would you like to check out the shops with me?"

"Good," I said, "I want to find something personal to take home for the girls. Maybe some crafted jewellery."

The shops were fun, not organized, neat and tidy like stores in the city. The spaces were small, and clothing, utensils, and everything crafty were piled hither and thither or hung from the ceiling. It was like being on a treasure hunt and finding interesting things. "Look at this dog collar," David near shouted. "Jewel studded. Isn't it a beauty?"

"A crown for a prince. Won't he look handsome." I winked at David and added, "Like his master."

"Be serious, Fiza," he said, and kissed my forehead. "Oh look, a dog coat. It ties on like a horse blanket. For winter. What do you think?"

"Is there a yellow one? You'd want it to match the jewels. I love these necklaces with a semi-precious stone pendant. I can't decide which one would suit Sue."

"The blue one," David replied without hesitation. "It'll match her eyes."

"How do you know her eye colour?" I teased, giving his arm a squeeze.

"Haven't you noticed? No one talks with their eyes more than she does."

"I hadn't noticed. She doesn't flirt with me. Oh look! A stained-glass butterfly windchime. Mom would love it." We went wild, buying far more than we intended. "We'll probably sink the ferry," I said, laughing. At the end of the row of shops stood a small building. Its siding boards were painted black and white like piano keys. On the bright blue door was a sign: Saturday Music Lessons. Come in and browse. I'll be right with you.

"Let's take a peek," David suggested, setting his parcels on the wooden bench by the door. I raised my eyebrow. "Not to worry. We'll only be a minute. This is a friendly island, not Manhattan." I surrendered my treasures to the bench, and we went in.

Musical instruments hung from every wall. There were African drums, and I spotted a zither. "Look, David," I exclaimed, "I haven't seen one of those in eons." I don't know if he heard me; he was listening to a young boy, about twelve with long hair, playing a guitar. An elderly man, wearing a scholar's jacket, used a stick to point out notes on the sheet music for his student.

A tiny, pot-bellied wood stove sat in the centre of the room. The counter was piled high with sheets and books of music. An old wooden milk bucket overflowed with instrument picks.

"Listen," David said. "That's it. Fiza, that's it."

The elderly man came over. "Can I be of help?' he asked.

"I'm looking to buy a guitar," David said.

"What do you have in mind? Take some off the wall. Hold them. See if anything suits you,"

"That won't be necessary," David said. "I would like to try the one the boy's playing."

The boy must have overheard the conversation. He stopped playing, stood up, and handed David the guitar. "It's not mine," he said. "It belongs to the shop."

David measured its heft, set it down. "What are you trying to feel, David?" I asked.

"Everything." He picked it up again, holding it in the playing position.

"Are you caressing it?" I asked.

"Yes. A good guitar is like a beautiful woman. You must be gentle." He fingerpicked the strings, strummed a few chords.

"Do you like the sound?" the elderly man asked.

"May I play a tune?"

"Of course."

David played, and he surprized us by singing.

"Imagine no possessions
I wonder if you can
No need for greed or hunger
A brotherhood of man
Imagine all the people
Sharing all the world, you"[8]

We were in a tiny shed of a place, but the blend of music and voice rose to the ceiling as if we were in the splendour of a cathedral. It sent shivers

---

[8] John Lennon, studio album, 1971, Apple Records

up my spine. David and this guitar looked as if they were embraced in an intimate dance. The boy's mouth gaped open.

"You may say I'm a dreamer
But I'm not the only one
I hope someday you'll join us
And the world will live as one."[9]

"You're a master, sir," the elderly man commented.

"You have shown me that music is a gift to the world," the boy said. "Thank you."

"It was my pleasure," David said, and turned to the boy, "You have talent, son. You would please me if you never give up music. I would like to pay for a few of your lessons." He handed the boy some money.

The boy's eyes near popped out of his head. "Thank you very much, sir. I'll give it to my mom. She takes in laundry to pay for my lessons. Thank you."

David and the elderly man continued to chat. As I had suspected, he owned the shop. I went out to check on our parcels. When David came out, he smiled from ear to ear. He had added something else to carry. He had bought the guitar. "Well, don't just stand there staring," he said, "we have a ferry to catch."

---

[9] John Lennon, studio album, 1971, Apple Records

Scene Twenty-One
The Ride Back to Ornskoldsvik

"**D**o you think Prince will like the collar?" he asked on the drive home.

"You love him likes he's your child," I said.

"So?"

"Should I be jealous?"

"Yes. I'll take him for a long run as soon as I get home. Then I need to go check on my day job. Robert's been texting. Seems there's a problem, and they want my opinion."

"What is it, exactly, that you do? What kind of engineering?"

"I work in research. The company specializes in innovational technology. Today's problem has to do with fiber optics. Did you know that Sweden is known worldwide for its fast internet services?"

"I had no idea. You are full of surprises. I took you for a mechanical engineer, a gearhead, not a tech geek. Why didn't we have this conversation when you came to apply to put Gertrude together?"

"You didn't ask. What difference would it have made?"

"I would have told you that you were overqualified, and I couldn't afford you."

"That was precisely what I was trying to avoid. I was having doubts about my high-flying lifestyle and when I saw your ad in Starbucks, I thought, why not? Why not take on a challenge that I would love? That's why I didn't want to be on your payroll. I wanted a hobby, an escape from reality when I needed it. I didn't want another commitment. I know I handled it all badly. But look what happened."

"Are you sorry?"

"My guardian angel must have been with me that day in Starbucks. Pocketing that ad was the best thing that I have ever done. I've missed Gertie. I'm eager to see if she'll really work."

"Do you have doubts?" I asked.

"About Gertie? No. About you? No. I love you," he said, blowing me a kiss.

"I'm curious. Why did your company hire an American?"

"On paper, I look good. I've had a rich education, a masters, a PhD. As I've told you, if the army was paying, I stayed at school."

He turned to look at me. Maybe he was curious to see how I would react to that revelation.

"Keep your eyes on the road, Doctor David," I said, filling my words with love. "Why didn't you tell me I should call you doctor? Why didn't it say Dr. David Jones on your card?"

"Now that would be a hoot. In my mind, doctors heal people, not antique looms. Why didn't you tell me I should call you Cinderella? Yours is a Cinderella story, rags to riches. I'm eager to hear how you came to Sweden. Let me see what's going down at the office. I might be busy for a few days. Then, would you come to my place for dinner? I'm not a bad chef. I'll find cushions for the floor."

"David, dinner would be nice. I will have a lot of catching up to do at The Store. Just let me know."

As the landscape rolled on, thoughts twirled. *Why have I met this educated, complicated, interesting man, who says he can cook and who owns a dog that he is madly in love with*? "David," I asked, "how did Prince come to be yours?"

"The psychiatrist, Dr. Lund, here in Ornskoldsvik, recommended that I have a pet. She thought I needed something to take care of. In her words, I was too self-absorbed. I never had a pet as a kid because my mother claimed to be allergic and thinking about it as an adult, I couldn't imagine being tied down to the mess. But because Dr. Lund had recommended it, I gave owning a dog some thought. One day, when I was driving past what I referred to as the animal pound, I decided to go in. It was really called 'The Society for the Prevention of Cruelty to

Animals.' 'Do you have any dogs available for adoption?' I asked a young lady carrying cages dripping wet.

'Too many,' she answered. 'My name is Sally. Let me show you around. A litter of puppies came in recently. They are so cute. Come, I'll show you.'

"The puppies were jumping all over each other, nibling ears, tumbling on the fake grass. When they noticed me, they came romping towards the fence barrier, some even trying to climb it. I knelt on a foam mat, that Sally gave me, to have a closer look. A chocolate brown one, with a white cross forehead marking, came dashing awkwardly to me. Sally handed me a small treat to offer the puppy. It had such sad eyes and huge paws. I couldn't help myself; I picked it up and cuddled it.

'He has chosen you,' Sally explained. 'What do you think?'

'But I'm not prepared yet,' I said, while the puppy suckled on my fingers.

'No problem. Our pet shop right next door, which supports the organization, has everything you need. You can buy a cage. Elias will take care of you.'

"Fiza, you can't imagine. No one would ever be able to imagine."

"Imagine what, David? What can't I imagine?"

"When I left that store, I had dropped hundreds of dollars. Hundreds, I tell you. Dog pellets which had more vitamins than I knew existed, two bowls—one for food, one for water, a stand with holes to fit the bowls, a stack of papers for the pup to pee on, a collar, a leash, a toothbrush. Can you imagine? A doggie toothbrush. And a *How to Take Care of Your Pet* manual."

I tried to stifle a laugh.

"You can laugh all you like, but let me tell you, I had stepped into something very serious. In the hallway in my apartment, I felt embarrassed carrying all that stuff. I was praying no one would see me. However, my elderly neighbour, Naslund, sees everything. He opened his door and said, 'Well, there, and what do you have in the cage?'

'It's a puppy,' I blurted out, rushing past, trying to escape.

'Well, there,' Naslund said following me, 'let's have a look.'

"Nothing I could do but set everything down. Naslund took the puppy from the cage and cuddled him. 'He's shaking,' he said. 'He's not been long from his mother is my guess. You've probably shaken him up in that cage. Pick up your stuff. I'll carry him.'

"Now, what was I to do? At least Naslund hadn't laughed at all the paraphernalia. Best to rush him, with the puppy, and all my stuff into the apartment and close the door.

'I miss my dog. She was old, she died a few months ago,' Naslund said.

'I'm so sorry,' I said, thinking I knew where this puppy really belonged. But it had already captured my heart and it was mine.

'I know a lot about dogs. Don't hesitate to ask if you have any problems.'

"And the rest is history."

"What a nice man," I said.

"He's my dog-sitter. That's why I don't mind leaving Prince with him. He's in good hands, and I know my neighbor enjoys having him."

"And how did you bond with this puppy?"

"I had forgotten what it was like to feel something. I fought to feel anything. When he came to me at the shelter, I felt something. I don't know what it was, but it stirred my heart. Although, trying to take care of him, especially those first few weeks, drove me to the brink of insanity, the joy that stirred my heart grew. Every time I put him in his cage, especially at night, he whined. I slept on the recliner, holding him. But slowly, I think he learned to trust that I wouldn't abandon him, and he settled. When I started to train him, he sensed how pleased I was when he learned a new command. I know he tried his best to please me. When I gave him a treat and said, "good boy" he wiggled himself almost inside out with pleasure. I can't imagine life without him."

"I've never seen a human so close to his pet. You and Prince are something special. And yes, David," I said, "I think he'll like his new collar."

"Prince taught me how to feel and now, with you, my feelings flow naturally. For both of you, I'll be eternally grateful. I'm glad we had this weekend. Without this time away, I wonder how long it would have taken to get to where we're at. I feel very close to you, Fiza."

"Our time away was what I needed. I, finally, started talking about my past. I feel so much lighter. I'm looking forward to coming to dinner."

Scene Twenty-Two

He opened the door and, bowing, offered me his hand. "Do come in, Princess. Be my guest."

"Oh my!" I said. "Something smells delicious. What have you been up to in the kitchen?"

"Come! I'll give you a peek," he said, ushering me towards the wafts of meat cooking, in his open-floor-plan apartment. Lifting a tin-foiled covering, he announced, "This is a venison roast. It's resting."

"Yummy. How long must it rest? Just the sight of it has me drooling, so brown and crispy on the top. And the drippings are tempting." I dipped my finger in the oozing juices.

He caught my hand and licked my finger, "Sorry, my dear, you'll have to wait till the Yorkshire puddings are done. They're in the oven. Do you want to thicken the gravy or toss the salad?"

"I'm a salad gal," I said, picking up the utensils. Lined up beside a huge wooden bowl of greens were the additives.

"I rubbed the bowl with a garlic clove," he said. "Garlic, even if it is roasted, can be a bit overpowering in a salad. A whiff to the nose and a hint to the pallet, I always say."

He was right, I thought, *when he said he wasn't a bad chef. He's extraordinaire.* "Do all these cranberries and sliced strawberries go into the bowl?"

"Yes, I didn't make dessert. You're getting it in the salad. The roast should be well rested; I'll cut it."

When I finished with the salad, he asked me to set it on the table. I hadn't noticed, while working in the kitchen, the beautifully appointed table setting in the dining area. A dozen or more different-sized candles, of different shades of blue, centered a midnight blue cloth that had tiny, embroidered stars. The dinnerware sparkled white with blue circular rims. "Have I got the forks and knives in the right order?" he asked, coming into the area. His eyes twinkled. "Please Fiza, would you light the candles? Don't forget the ones in the wall sconces. They give a flickering warm glow. It's more romantic."

When we sat, I lifted my wine glass to him and said, "Skal, David. It's all so lovely. You've made such a grand effort. Thank you."

"Seeing as I have a table, I thought we should dine up off the floor," he said, jokingly. Then, more seriously, he added, "Skal, my Princess. It pleases me that you've come to my place. Bon Appetit."

"The venison melts in the mouth, and the flavour!" I brought my thumb and fingers to my lips and made a smacking sound. "Is the basting a David Jones well-kept secret?"

"Dijon mustard, thyme, red peppercorns. The secret is to roast it slowly."

"And you've roasted the asparagus. It's so full flavoured and crispy. I was taught to stand asparagus in a pot of boiling water with the heads poking upwards to catch the steam. And to smother the mushy finished product with butter. I like this drizzle. Don't tell me, you stole some of the Karaoke Café's famous Modena balsamic vinegar."

"You're so discerning and appreciative. It's fun to cook for you. When I took cooking lessons, I became enthusiastic. Choosing herbs to sprinkle or seeking for the best real vanilla at the market brings out some hidden creative gene."

"Any hidden creative gene, that I might have, doesn't stretch beyond roasting on a fire pit. I don't think Dijon mustard or red peppercorns were prevalent in the market of my youth. I should add cooking lessons to my to do list."

"Don't belittle yourself, Fiza. You did miracles, in your tiny kitchen, with that scrumptious cheese soufflé."

"Thank you, David. With your praise and this epicurean dinner, I'm satiated."

"Then, let's take coffee in the sitting room," he said, pushing back his chair and standing. Sorry, I didn't have time to get floor cushions, but you can take the ones off the sofa. I'll just be a few minutes."

"I would like to use the bathroom."

"Help yourself. The guest room is the door by the entrance. Be careful. Some of the paint may still be wet."

"Guest bathroom! An entire army could have fit in the pristine, pale blue and white, chandeliered space. Cinnamon and cloves puffed from an infuser. Painted male and female dancing figures took up an entire wall and were reflected in the mirrors. The male twirled the female away, her skirt flaring. His backwards thrusted leg kept the balance. Their eyes and hands held each other. *How beautiful. A moment of ecstasy caught in time.* It touched me that David had painted us here on the wall. I took my finger and traced the outline of the female figure. No mistaking. It had to be his interpretation of us dancing at the Karaoke Café. I started to shake. He had painted a crystal on his neck chain. I looked closer. *Yes, it was the lapis lazuli.* I never really knew what he had felt about my gift. Seeing it included in the painting brought tears to my eyes and sent shivers up my spine. I wondered if he had searched out its meaning, strength and courage, royalty and wisdom, intellect, and truth.

To bring myself back to the moment, I took in the rest of the room. The cobalt and blue-grey accents—the mats, below the two above-counter sinks, with images of antique cars, the pull-blind with sky-blue musical notes and lyrics—saved the room from looking feminine. I walked over to the blind. Sure enough, "Lara's Theme" was there. *Even down to the minutest detail. "Lara's theme" has become our song.* My heart swelled. I splashed my face with cool water and dried on a towel from the warmer.

I stood for a minute or so, to regain my balance, then went to arrange the cushions.

With an ear-to-ear grin and a twinkle in his eyes that lit up to the lofty ceilings, he handed me my coffee. At first, I didn't realize what was giving him such pleasure, but then I noticed a picture of the almost-finished Gertrude printed on the mug. "Oh, David!"

"It's yours. I thought you might like to add it to your mugs. What was it that you called it? Oh yes, now I remember. Your Storied Collection."

"Thank you, David. It not only shows your devotion to the loom, but it tells me that you are accepting me, even with my oddities."

"I've grown fond of sitting on the floor."

"I like your place. Everything about it says David." I knew no one else could have painted us, so truly us, but I asked, "Did you paint the picture in the guest bathroom?"

"Yes. Did you notice the only things painted brown in the picture?" he asked.

"No."

"You're not very observant," he said, grinning. "Let's go have a look."

"It's the eyes," I said, as we walked back to the sitting area and settled on the cushions.

"We know why you have such beautiful brown eyes," he said, "but why have you never asked why my eyes are so dark?"

"Racial features were never on the agenda," I said, "but if you wish, I'll ask."

"Please," he said, "I would like you to."

"Why are your eyes so dark?"

"My mother was African American."

"Did you also inherit her rhythm?" I asked, recalling how enchanted I was when watching David run and dance.

"And her tinge of melanin and her voice."

He reached beside the sofa and picked up the guitar he had bought on the Island.

"I had forgotten, until I got this guitar, how music sings to my soul," he said, strumming. He sang Lara's Theme.[10]

> **"Somewhere my love there will be songs to sing**
> **Although the snow covers the hope of Spring**
> **Somewhere a hill blossoms in green and gold**
> **And there are dreams, all that your heart can hold."**

---

[10] Dr. Zhivago: Lara's Theme

If his eyes were the mirror of his soul, I could see right into it and hear the echoes of its singing. His voice had me trembling. My heart vibrated. I felt like I had grown gossamer wings and would, at any moment, fly off into the ethers. It was so reminiscent of our first date when he sang to me at the Karaoke Café.

"You've thought of everything," I said. "Thank you so much. You have made this a very special evening."

Scene Twenty-Three

The Picnic

On Saturday, when I went to Gertrude's Place, David was already in the kitchen. Excitement bounced off the walls. "We're playing hooky," he said, practically jumping up and down. "Are we celebrating? Is it your birthday?" I asked.

"I was born sometime in the winter, I think," he said, a flashback to my 'sometime in spring'. It pleased me that he had remembered that conversation. We had gone for lunch at a beach side café, and he had asked me when my birthday was. That had to be four months ago. *Oh gosh. It's August already.* "I've packed a picnic basket. I thought we could go to Grove Park, hike the trail to the Old Waterwheel, come back and eat under the oaks. Prince will love the free run among the trees. Quick, go get those 'pineapples' you bought on the Islands. You can test whether the spiky yellow soles are as grippy as the shop keeper claimed. I'll give Prince a drink and meet you at the car. And bring a light jacket, it might get chilly."

"Ooof," was my retort to his calling my hiking boots, 'pineapples.' "They're vegan," I added, "that means a lot to me." *Spontaneous,* I thought as I changed into my boots and athletic wear. I had heard that the Grove Grind wasn't an easy walk in the park. *Just like that. Fun injected into routine. Why not?*

Before we started on the Grind, we read the sign. Difficulty—challenging. Length—2.5 km. Elevation gain—500 meters. Bring water + snack + mobile phone. Today's sightings–two cougars some distance from trail—be alert. "Are you sure, David, that we want to do this?" I asked, stepping away from the sign and clinging to his arm.

"It's up to you. Prince will frighten off any animals if that's your concern. We don't have to do the whole thing. We can come back down whenever you wish."

"Okay. I'm game. I need the exercise and the fresh air. Let's go," I said.

We walked, stopping often to drink, even sitting on some of the stone steps to rest and breathe in the scent of pine. Prince dashed back and forth through the tall coniferous trees, scaring a few partridges but, as far as we were aware, didn't have to frighten any cougars. When we neared the top, David took my hand, "How are you doing?"

"A little wobbly in the legs," I answered, "but I feel great."

We reached the Old Waterwheel. Its look was of antiquity. I thought of the beloved book, *The Mill on the Floss.* If I remember correctly, it was first published in 1860.

Using our last bit of energy, we jumped up and down screeching, "We did it. We did it." You would think that we had just summitted the Himalayas. Prince walked into the creek that ran under the wheel and took a long drink. David and I hugged, then sat on the Heroes Bench to take in the view. White clouds danced above the city.

"From here," I commented, "It looks like a fairyland. My whole body is saying that we should sit here until the end of time. What do you say, David?"

"I agree. This is a most enchanting view of Ornskoldsvik. But my stomach says we had better find our way down before I starve to death."

On the way down, my legs cramped. Not enough to stop and massage, but the thought, *I'll feel every muscle tomorrow*, came often.

When we got back to the oaks, we collapsed on a park bench, to catch our breath and to recover. Prince paddled in a near-by creek.

"I'm proud of us," David said. "We our mountaineers extraordinaire."

"I'm not so sure about this mountaineer. Time will tell. Perhaps it was a little much for a first time. I'll shake out the blanket while you set out Prince's food."

"Come Prince," he called when the food was ready.

"A different army surplus?" I commented, arranging the blanket under the trees.

"And one day soon, it'll be one of Gertie's," he answered.

"Oh, David, won't that be exciting!"

"We should bring it here to celebrate," he added. "Champagne, Gertie's first blanket, and you. Could a man have it any better?"

He opened the picnic basket.

"Oh my! You've packed the entire kitchen," I said. "You certainly are a man of many talents."

He spread a white tablecloth on the blanket between us. "Venison spread with David's special mustard, thyme, and red peppercorn sauce, sprinkled with cilantro sprigs," he said, placing the filled, fresh croissants in the center of the cloth. "Crisp cucumber salad and sweet apple quarters," he announced, setting them across from the croissants. "And triangles of sharp cheddar cheese, to make up the point. I present my **heart** for your taking, my love."

"The presentation is grand. You've touched me, but is it just for looking at? I'm starved."

"Of course not, let's dig in. Would you like some sparkling water?" he asked, presenting a steel bottle.

He's been so thoughtful and kind. He's learned how harmful it is to keep traumatic things hidden. He's felt my pain and is doing everything to help me. Who could ask for a better man?

When we had eaten our fill, David said, "There's hot coffee in the thermos, and I baked lemon tarts, but let's wait a bit. I brought you here for a reason."

"May I ask what that might be?"

"I ear-marked where your story left off. You seem to be skirting around it. I thought perhaps, out here, you might continue. That is, if you don't think I'm being intrusive."

"Thank you, David. That's thoughtful of you. It's been circling, nonstop. I want to get it out. I need to get it out. I thought I might talk last night, but I was overcome by the effort you'd made to show me that you cared. I was too emotional. I couldn't even tell you how much your painting in the guest bathroom moved me. What a relief it was when I saw the coffee mug. It roiled my emotions, but it wasn't so heavy. Where did I leave off with my story?"

"You had come back from the camp and were at your aunt's. She had just told you that your family was dead."

"Your eyes seem eager," I said, stalling. The mention of my family stung my eyes and caught in my throat. I lost the coherence of our conversation.

"If I seem eager, Fiza, it's because I don't think you should leave your story at that point. I want to hear what transformed you."

"Where to start?" I asked.

"Don't think about it. It's best to just start talking," he said.

"As you can imagine, my aunt was at her wits end with worry over me," I said.

I paused. After a few moments, I was able to continue.

"One day, although she had no way of knowing whether it was a good idea, she asked me to come with her to the other side of the village. 'I think it's time,' she said, 'to go see if the tree is still there.'"

I took a few deep breaths.

"No one had built a tukul on Father's land. Grasses flourished there. Some bent. Some swaying in the breezes. It was as if Father's land had returned to the wild."

There was a stinging behind my eyes, but determined to tell it all, I fought back the tears.

"I flung myself on the grass and cried out, 'Please Father, come and get me. Please Father, take me. I want to be with the children. Please Father. Please. Please. Someone help me. Anyone. I need help.'"

Tears came uncontrollably. I twisted up into a ball and sobbed.

David put his arms around me. "Cry it out, love. You're safe. I'm here. Cry it out." His words soothed me, and I uncoiled. We lay on the blanket holding each other.

Eventually, I said, "There on the grass, having grieved, I curled up. My aunt comforted me with soothing words and then said, 'Rest a while, my child. I'll visit others I haven't seen in some time, and then I'll come back for you.' Exhausted, I fell asleep."

"What about your father's tree?" David asked. "Was it still there?"

"Yes, it was. I could barely recognize it. It had grown twice my height."

"Thank you, Fiza for sharing your story with me. I know it was difficult for you. It took a lot of courage. I felt your pain."

"It's been in my head for a very long time. I needed to say it out loud. Thank you for encouraging me and listening. Shall we have coffee? And didn't you mention something about a freshly baked tart?"

"That I did. I'll get the tarts. Would you pour the coffee?"

When we were sitting up, drinking our coffee, I said, "I love this tart. It leaves the squeeze of lemon on my tongue."

"Squeeze of lemon," he remarked. "Well, that's intriguing."

"Lemon lifts my spirits. I'm feeling good. This picnic was a marvelous idea. I'll let you know tomorrow how I feel about the hike. It'll depend on whether my legs let me get out of bed."

"I'm depending on you. It takes two to do the testing Gertie needs."

"David, I want to tell you how I came to leave South Sudan. How I ended up here in Sweden. Can you come to dinner at the turret next week?"

"I have an off day on Wednesday. Will that work for you?"

"Wednesday it is."

Scene Twenty-Four
Buried Traumas

I loved hearing his footsteps bounding up the stairs. No matter what happens between us, I'll carry that sound forever. It says, with joy, *Here I am, all of me, just for you.* Perhaps I love that sound because it is in counterpoint to something deep in me that fears being abandoned.

"Black pansies," he said with the excitement of a six-year-old offering the greatest present to his mother. I liked how the innocence of a child, which was probably thwarted after his sister's death, shows up in him. He thrusted a bouquet of three flowers, wrapped in a filigree of miniature lacy fern, at me. "They represent sorrow, but also a deep yearning for everlasting love."

"That's beautiful." I said, and my eyes watered. Smelling the pansies, I added, "They have such a delicate spicy fragrance. They're lovely. Thank you."

"They are spring plants. You can't imagine the effort I've made finding these in August. The florist tried to convince me that they are not used in bouquets, but I turned on my charm and, finally, she cut a few from a potted plant. I'm starving. The moment I stepped out of the car I could smell Italian. Spaghetti? I hope you've protected your cushions. You know how inept I am with chopsticks." He chatted on, enjoying our insider's joke that stemmed from a Chinese take-out episode. He gathered me in his arms. "Let me dance you to the kitchen."

"My, aren't you in a bouncy mood. So wordy. If I didn't know better, I would think you had spent the day at the pub."

"Cupid's arrow has been striking me all day. I'm on a high."

I had to be quick to protect the flowers, holding them behind his back. "We need to find something special — precious cut glass, an antique vase – only the best for black pansies," I said.

We settled on a simple Japanese porcelain container.

"It complements perfectly," David said, "and doesn't steal the show from the flowers." Because he had noticed that the windowsill was set as a table, he placed the flowers there. "I see you've brought stools from The Store," he said. "This is a change."

"Sometimes we need to look at life from a different perspective. Would you grate the parmesan, please?"

I had scrunched fresh tomatoes in basil, parsley, thyme, and rosemary spices and let the sauce simmer for hours before adding the sautéed onions, garlic, and chicken pieces. I ladled it over spaghetti on plates. I knew that David liked cucumber salad, so I had picked some up at the deli when I was at the bakery for fresh focaccia.

"You make the best tomato sauce in all of Ornskoldsvik," David commented, twirling his spaghetti in his spoon. "And the view from here is spectacular. I can see a cruise ship coming in."

We ate, watching the sun set, until the city was lost to us, then we took our latte macchiatos and sat on the cushions.

When I was feeling comfortable, I asked, "Can I tell you what I remember about leaving my village?"

"If you're ready, Fiza."

"Maybe it was a miracle," I said. "Maybe it was Father's way of helping me. I'll never know, but when my aunt and I were returning from visiting Father's place, from a distance, we could make out two people standing outside her tukul. When we approached, her neighbor spoke, 'The doctor has a proposal for Fiza. He works at the hospital. Come, Fiza, and hear what he has to say.'

"I stood in front of the doctor. To show respect, I lowered my eyes for a few moments. When I raised them, I was struck with the strange feeling that I had seen him before, but it wouldn't come to me. 'Fiza', he asked, 'do you recognize me?'

"It was his voice, that triggered a memory, and I shrieked. 'I thought you were dead. Didn't they shoot you?'

"David, I'm so amazed that I remember that conversation. That doctor was from the terrorist's camp where the kidnappers took me. But I can't remember anything else about that camp. I was told later that I had helped the doctor, and he had come to repay me. I want to tell you the outcome of that conversation."

"Please, Fiza, I want to know what happened."

"The doctor offered to take me to live with him and his wife, who was also a doctor at the hospital. They wanted me to train as a midwife.

"I went into my aunt's tukul, put all my belongings in a carrying sack, came out, and started up the path out of the village. My God, David, how strange. I now remember it all as if it happened yesterday. I don't mean the camp. I'm talking about what happened that day when I left my village. The doctor rushed after me, trying to keep up. I can still see the ladies waving from the peanut fields."

"My psychiatrist calls it *selective memory*. I don't think we select to forget. I believe that some traumas are so devastating that we couldn't live unless we blocked them," David said.

I went pensive. Thoughts bounced everywhere. *Why have I blocked out the camp? What traumas did I need to bury?* I felt sick. Dizziness clouded my thinking. Hidden in this mess, I intuited, was the reason I couldn't be intimate with men. If I wanted to have love everlasting with David, I knew, no matter how devastating it might be, that I had to remember what happened to me in that camp and somehow come to terms with it.

I took a deep breath, and with great effort said, "Do you think it was a survival tactic? Do you think I blocked out what happened in the camp so I could live?"

"I don't know," he said, "but it wouldn't surprise me. Why don't you seek a therapeutic analysis? Or maybe a psychiatrist?"

"I've tried all that. And tantric yoga. And meditation. Deep breathing. Hanging up-side-down. You've seen what you called 'that contraption.' Name it; I've tried it. I know it's all meant to take me back to re-live my trauma, but I stop short. I don't know if it's because I don't want to embarrass myself in front of a therapist or if I'm afraid that the pain will be too much, but I've become an expert at stalling and diverting. Perhaps, to survive, I need to keep it hidden.

"When I went up the trail out of my village," I continued, "I never looked back. Now, whenever I think of my village, of my family, of Father's tukul, in my mind I see only smoke rising. My pain, my sorrow, all my lost love, I've packaged into that one scene."

His eyes filled with sadness and they were outlined with the dearest compassion I've ever felt.

"David," I said, "people say that every life is braided with luminous moments. I try to think of the moment when I walked out of my village as luminous. It was the beginning of a wonderful life that I couldn't have imagined. I've practiced visualization for a long time. When I think of that luminous moment, I visualize wild butterflies. A sky full of beautiful wild butterflies, all the colors of the rainbow."

"That's beautiful."

"But grey smoke rising, inevitably, comes back."

"Fiza, I'm sorry."

I didn't want his pity; and he never gave it. His *sorry* was filled with sympathy and care. Hugging him, I said, "Nonetheless, David, in that parched earth of my life, in that luminous moment, wells of possibilities begin to spring up, and here I am. This has become all too heavy. Let's go up to the shop. You haven't seen my invention... blue dye."

"Let's take the long way. There's a full moon. It always sheds light on shrouded darkness," he said.

When we arrived at The Store, a dozen boxes had been delivered. David and I, forgetting all about my invention, spent hours unpacking and lining the shelves in the dyeing room with large wooden spools of colored yarns. "You've chosen beautiful colours, Fiza," David remarked. "I can hardly wait to see how you want the loom set to make the blankets you have envisioned."

"Stripes of various widths," I said. "The colours complementing. The completion of a dream."

Scene Twenty-Five
Polaris Speaks

I was excited about the yarn that had arrived. *It's one step closer to fulfilling the dream I hold for the loom*, I thought, but the queasiness from my talking about the past still lingered in my gut. Questions still churned. *Why have I blocked out the camp? What traumas did I need to bury?* Although I was exhausted from the unpacking, I couldn't sleep. Even when I closed my eyes, I saw grey smoke. I felt like a tapped maple tree. I had come to the end of my season, void of anything life-giving.

I started questioning my life. Does The Store and this, probably unfulfillable dream of producing heirloom blankets, have me stuck? Why does every encounter I have with men rattle some chains in my memory, stir up anxiety, inhibit me. *What do I fear?*

My soul stripped bare; I went to the window. The stars vibrated. I found Polaris, Grampa Y's star. I sensed an uncomfortable thought. It came to me from the star's vibrations, shapeless, undefined. Then it formed into words: *I must go back. I must go to my village. I must go through the hole in the fence and look where the camp was.* The last was the strangest; I didn't remember any hole in the fence. Those thoughts came to me not just with certainty, but with a strong scent of poinciana blossoms and poignant lemon. Was it Grampa's intervention? Was it my subconscious mind? I did not know which, but I decided to go to South Sudan. The sooner, the better.

I taped a calendar on the fridge door, then marked September 30 with a big X. In one month, I was going to South Sudan. I was in for the full send—the act of irreversibly going all out regardless of the consequences. I was willing to do what I must, to have a loving, fulfilling relationship with David. I wanted the whole package—lover, wife, mother, the happily-ever-after.

David had told me that he also wants the whole package with me, children playing in a large backyard. *I wonder how he'll react when I tell him I'm going to Africa?*

Scene Twenty-Six
A Proposal

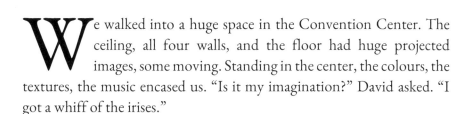

We walked into a huge space in the Convention Center. The ceiling, all four walls, and the floor had huge projected images, some moving. Standing in the center, the colours, the textures, the music encased us. "Is it my imagination?" David asked. "I got a whiff of the irises."

"Perchance," I answered. "This is supposed to be total immersion. It's certainly nothing like going to an art gallery and viewing one of Van Gogh's famous paintings."

"I had no idea that he was so productive. I'm loving this. A whole semester of art classes in one evening," David commented. "Which painting is your favourite?"

"The Potato Eaters," I said. "There's something about people sharing food that touches a deep part of me. In the painting they are feasting on the simple potato, and it feels like a celebration. Do you have a favourite?"

"I'm drawn to the self-portraits. Not the one where he's cut off his ear. I don't want to think that such a creative man could be mentally ill. I like the one where he's wearing the brimmed straw hat. Because it's blown up so large, his eyes pierce me to my very soul. No matter where I walk, those eyes follow me. They're haunting. I hope Gertie never ends up in a dusty old museum."

"Where did that come from?" I asked.

"I don't know. I haven't been to many art galleries; I've always thought of them as museums for old paintings and the thought came to me that the loom is antique."

"Never you busy your mind with thoughts like that. You will have Gertrude up and running any time now. When you get the timing mechanisms correlated, we'll set a simple pattern and do some trial runs. She will show the world that an antique loom shouldn't end up in any old museum."

"The timing mechanisms are the most delicate. Every time I adjust them, I must turn on the loom to test. I hold the lever, so I can immediately shut it off if things aren't right. I don't want to cause a lot of damage. That might set us back, God knows how long."

When we came out, I felt that something had changed in us, that we had moved on from thoughts about me and my past. *When will I get a chance to tell him that I'm going to South Sudan?* Do you want to come up for coffee?" I asked, as we walked the short distance to the turret.

He stood at the window, taking in the view, while I made coffee. When I handed him his, he inspected the mug, "This is Van Gogh's *Irises*. I'm so proud of myself. After the immersion, I think I'll always recognize his art."

"Wrap your hands around it. Get the full feel." I laughed.

Then, being serious, I said, "David, ever since our last talk, I've thought about you and me." I paused, tongue-tied. He looked at me, quizzically. I took a breath, and said, "You might think this is crazy, but... I want nothing more than for you and me to be the ones in that house with children and the apple tree in the yard." *God Fiza, that's not what you wanted to say. Don't stall. Just say it.*

"What is so crazy about that? Surely you know that is also my dream."

"No, David, that's not the crazy part. Please hear me out." I breathed deeply. "I need to go to South Sudan. I need to go back to my village and to where that camp was. Perhaps there, my memories will come back to me. I must find out what happened to me in that camp. If I can come to terms with whatever that was, then you and I will have a better chance to have the life together that we both dream of. I know, deep in my bones, that my journey must take this path backwards to give me the possibility to move forwards."

I'll never forget the look on his face. It was the look of a little boy whose mother walked out on him. *Had I given him a flash back to his childhood and being abandoned by his mother?*

"Give me time, Fiza," he said. "I need to have time to think about what you've just said. Right now, my mind can't think about you leaving me. I'm scared. What if you don't come back? What if I lose you?"

"David, you've gotten beyond thinking about yourself. You care for Prince. You love him. Since I gave you a second chance, your attitude towards me has changed. You go out of your way not to make everything about you. It's now about you and me. Please don't revert to your old way of thinking. *What about **me** if you don't come back? What about **me** if I lose you?* You've shown me that you're a much bigger man than that. It's highly unlikely that I won't come back. We must trust the universe. I'm scared. I'll never say that I'm not, but for us, for our future happiness, I'm willing to risk it. I love you. Can you take this risk with me? Are you strong enough to not let this slip you back into depression?"

I never took my eyes off him. He sat so still I thought he might have turned into a statue. "You're right. I must not think that this is about me and how I feel," he said. "It's about what you need to do, and I will support you." He fiddled with his watch in a way that I now knew that he wanted to say more, so I waited, then he met my eyes. "You've taught me that to live without love is not to live at all. I've come to love you to the depths of the deepest oceans and to the heights of the highest mountains. Because I love you so deeply, the more I'll be hurt if I lose you, but... Fiza, I'm strong enough. I'm willing to take the risk. Why don't we go down to the sea and walk barefoot in the sand?"

On our way, David said, "Whenever I'm off balance, I'm drawn to the sea. Its distinct rhythm is order; but it is also wildness. Its cadence speaks to me."

"That's beautiful, David. You grew up inland. I'm so happy that you've come to enjoy the sea. Look how the moon shimmers across the water." We took off our shoes and, holding hands, ran into the shallow water. The effort soon had me winded. David noticed. Pretending to slip, he pulled me out of the water, down onto the sand. "Have you ever made sand angels?" I asked.

"No. But I'm not above trying." Two adults, fully clothed, flapping in the sand. We stood up and looked at our artwork. "Your wings might be the prettiest but mine are the biggest," he said, laughing. "Race you into the water." In the water, we got into a water fight, splashing with fury. You'd think we were trying to drown each other. We fell at the edge, laughing and rolled over into a hug. He held me tight. I wasn't sure what his strong embrace was trying to express. *Is he saying, don't go? Does he want me to remember that I'm his?* "What is this thing called love?" he asked, releasing me.

"It's David and Fiza, out of their minds, acting like kids," I said.

"Because," he said, "we're making up for a lost childhood that neither of us had. I've let you in Fiza. Now I'm never going to let you out."

"Thank you, David. I don't want out. I feel secure with you."

"You allow me to imagine a day when our heart scars will be invisible. I'm willing to do whatever it takes. I'm all in for you, Fiza," he said.

"Thank you, David. I'm counting on that. I wouldn't be able to do it without your support. Let's go home and have a hot shower."

"Together?"

"Together."

"I would like to stay the night. May I stay over?" he asked. Before I could answer, he went on, "And tomorrow, after you've made me breakfast," he said with a wink, "we'll plan your trip. The sooner we get you there, the sooner you'll get back. And Fiza, let's get married."

"Slow down, David. You've gone from a stay over, to breakfast, and that last bit sounded like a proposal."

"It is. Laying in the sand isn't exactly like kneeling, but it's sincere. I assure you, Fiza, I'm sincere. What do you say?"

"I say that would make me the happiest person in the entire universe." I kissed him. He kissed me. We smothered each other in kisses. "I love you, David. I love you so much. And I'm sincere."

"Love is proposing to the one you love, to the moon and back, while lying in the sand with the tide washing up to us," he said. "I would like to seal my promise to you." He took a ring off his little finger and showed it to me. "It was my mother's engagement ring. The stone is a ruby. Would you accept it?"

"David," I whispered, tears rolling down my face, "I accept." He slipped the ring on my finger and kissed my tears away. We held each other in an embrace that spoke more than words could express. It said, I'll treasure you forever, love without ending. On this day, August 30th, forward, I promise to do my best for **us.** I held my hand so the moon could shine on the ring. "Oh, how beautiful," I said. "So beautiful."

"Now that you're my fiancé, do I get to use your lavender shampoo?"

Scene Twenty-Seven
Who Knows?

"I haven't been home to South Sudan since I was a child," I told the librarian. "Now, I'm planning a trip, and I want to catch up. Can you recommend some books that might help me understand what has been happening in my country?"

"Oh, how interesting. I love it when people want to do research before embarking on trips. I've never been, but I've set up an entire section on Africa. Come, let's have a look."

"My," I said, when we reached the aisle, "so many books. Are any specifically on South Sudan?"

"This is the best," she said, handing me Hilde F. Johnson's *South Sudan*[11]. It'll give you the background you need to understand the terrible state that South Sudan is still in."

"Thank you. I don't only want to know the politics; do you have any books by Sudanese authors?"

"This anthology, *Modern Sudanese Poetry*, might give you a feel for your country and its people. It's a good bedside companion. Just open it to any page and read the poem. Let the poem settle with you before moving to another. Take the book and see what you think. If you like it, may I suggest you buy a copy and take it with you on your trip."

"What a good idea. I'm leaving at the end of the month, so I haven't much time. Is there anything else you would suggest?

---

[11] Hilde F. Johnson, South Sudan: The Untold Story, I.B. Taris & Co. Limited, 2018.

"Taban Io Liyong, who was born in South Sudan, is a prolific writer of highly imaginative short narratives, many about Sudan. He's a scholar. He's taught in many countries, but now he's at the University of Juba."

"I'm going to Juba. Hopefully, I'll get to the University. Perhaps, I'll meet this author. You've been terrific. Thank you so much."

"If I don't see you before you go, have a great trip, and come by and tell me all about it when you return."

While I was deep into Hilde F. Johnson's book, David was a great help. He spent hours on the phone trying to research flights. The connections proved difficult. He didn't want me stuck in airports for hours. When he was on hold, which was often, we chatted. "Have you been in touch with your aunt that helped you?" he asked. "You said she was your father's sister. What's her name?"

"I just called her Auntie. As children we never called our elders by first names. I am ashamed to say, since the day I left, I haven't once tried to get in touch with her. I don't know if she's still alive, but I have a gold necklace and an envelope of currency for her."

"I have to know where you are and how to get in touch with you."

"David," I said, "I think you know that Dad, before he came to Sweden and brought me with him, was a doctor in the hospital in Juda. He's been in touch with his contact there. The hospital will house me and give me a job in the Midwife Ward until I settle. I worked in that ward for a while before I left Juda, and I've been to the Midwife Ward, here at the hospital, to prepare myself."

"I've finally got it straight," he said, "when you say Dad you mean your adopted Dad. You always refer to your biological father as Father. My God, Fiza. It sounds so disorganized. That's not how it worked in the army. Everything was planned to the nth degree. I'm worried."

"David, I'll do my best to be ready, but I can't tell you exactly how things will work out. I won't know until I get there. I don't want you to worry. I'll keep in touch with you as best I can, and you'll know the decisions I make."

I didn't tell him that South Sudan didn't function like the U.S. army. I didn't tell him all the things that I was unsure of. I might stay at the hospital and never go to the village. Perhaps I'll stay at the hospital and make periodic visits to the village. There's a chance that I'll stay in my village, indefinitely. If I find what I'm looking for, I may be satisfied and return to Sweden quite soon. Perchance, I'll learn what is good to remember and what is better to forget. I just didn't know.

Scene Twenty-Eight
Decision Day

The fog crept up from the sea, sneaking between the houses to get to me at the window in my turret. I didn't mind. It's an enigmatic kind of day. Today's the day for a final decision. Tomorrow, I must confirm my flights. Will I go to South Sudan, or not?

Mom and Dad invited us for dinner. Sister Ellie would be there. "You can tell us what you've decided, Fiza," Mom said. "We're all anxious to know."

At dinner the talk was all about food, but after, over coffee in the sitting room, it became eclectic. Any topic was up for grabs. Sister Ellie, who was home from Trinity College doing a specialty in oncology at the hospital, said, "My head is full of 'the latest breakthroughs' in medicine, the newest technologies, but something puzzles me."

"What puzzles you?" Dad asked.

"Why haven't I learned how to heal sick people?"

"Age-old question," Mom said. "You, Ellie, are wise beyond your training years. It took me a long time, as a practicing doctor, to realize that patients heal themselves; or they do not. If anything, I do no more than shift how they live their life. Hopefully, it's for the better."

"Maybe I need to go with Fiza," Ellie said. "I could be exposed to grassroots patient care. I would find that more gratifying than pushing buttons and prescribing pills."

"Medicine's saga covers millennia," Dad started with his wise words that we all loved to hear. "Everything depends on where your bookmark is placed. You might go into the villages, Ellie and learn what plants are used for what. That's grassroots. But you've had enough training; you know that a certain pill is a concentrated form of what is found in those plants. It's the economy of the whole business that gets to me, globalized economics, but we could talk about that until the cows come home and never change anything. This is not the time for you to quit your specialty. Finish it. Get some experience under your belt, then decide what path you'll take."

"I know, Dad," Ellie said. "It's just that Fiza has pushed some restless buttons in me. I've done my best to delay what you are here to tell us, Fiza. I want to know, and I don't want to know. But now, I can't control the pins and needles any longer. Please, Fiza. What is your final decision?"

Dad intervened with, "I realize it's risky, but if you've decided to go, Fiza, I'll support you."

"Thank you, Dad. I know I can count on you." I saw fear in my mom's blanched face, so I put my arms around her, and said, "I want you to know, Mom, you've always been my inspiration. You helped me accept the loss of my family by sharing how you felt growing up without a father. You encouraged me through my struggles to learn English. You supported me through my career aspirations. You walked me into independence by approving my move to the turret. When I told you that I needed to try and unlock things I had hidden from my past you said, 'Fiza, you must listen to your inner voice and do what you need to do.' That, Mom, was all the inspiration I needed."

"I might have provided inspiration," Mom said, "but I cannot provide courage. You must look into your own soul for that."

"When I need courage, Mom, I just have to think of you."

"If you are going, Fiza. I want to go with you," Ellie said. "I wish to see the tree that everyone tells me, Dad, that you planted for me when I was born. I know Dad; I know what you'll say about that; It's not your time. So, Fiza, if you go, you must give me a full report on my tree. Promise."

"And, David, the girls at The Store tell me if Fiza goes to South Sudan, they won't leave you alone to crawl back into your shell. They expect you to come to The Store, work on Gertrude if you wish, and to bring them coffee, and tell them whatever you've heard from Fiza," Mom said, twisting a hankie, trying to control her emotions.

"Thank you, Mrs. Doc," David said. "I'm not sure that I want to work on the loom without Fiza. There's some puttering to be done, but I won't start any weaving without her. It's her project."

"And don't make yourself scarce around here, David," Dad added. Like Mom, he thought he knew my decision, and was trying to be brave. "Or are you afraid my timing at the racetrack is going to get better than yours?"

"You all talk as if you know what I've decided. And you are right. I'm going to South Sudan," I said.

"Then we must drink to a successful trip and a safe homecoming," Dad announced. "Ellie, bring the glasses. David, if you can help me with this cork, I'll pour."

They lifted their glasses to me, "Skal. Safe and happy journey."

"I appreciate all your support. Thank you," I whispered, through a huge lump that had caught in my throat.

"May I make another announcement?" David asked, rescuing me from my threatening tears.

"Don't tell me you're going with Fiza?" Ellie exclaimed.

"Wait," Dad said, "Let David have his say. Well, David?"

"Fiza and I are engaged," he said. I held out my hand to show my ring.

Ellie rushed over to have a closer look. "Oh, how beautiful," she said, and hugged me. "I'm so happy for the two of you, and you're the luckiest man on the planet, David," she added, hugging him. "And Fiza has hit the jackpot."

"Well, then, this calls for another toast," Dad said. "Lift your glasses to Fiza and David. To your happiness."

"Skal."

"It pleases me," Mom added, hugging us. "A ruby stone is affiliated with fortune, happiness, and love. I wish you the best in everything."

"I appreciate everyone's approval," David said. "It means everything to me." He went over and shook Dad's hand.

"I don't need to say, welcome to our family," Dad said, "because you've been a part of us for some time already, David, but I'm happy that you wish to make it formal. But don't expect another handicap on the racetrack."

The evening had been so emotionally packed that when we finally had coffee, everyone went *swoosh* and settled back, exhausted. The conversation settled on mundane utterings about the weather and the latest entertainment around town.

It wasn't lost on me that within this unit, called family, that I was supported in two new pages of my life. One page was my past, which would hopefully allow a second page, as an engaged woman who would be able to find happiness in marriage.

David and I said our goodnights and went out into a pleasant evening. It was early September and Ornskoldsvik was enjoying a much-appreciated Indian summer. We walked the long way home, taking in the gentle harvest breeze, counting stars as they appeared in the clear sky. I said to David, "You and I have climbed mountains. At other times, we have dug ourselves out of deep holes. Do you think we'll ever find flat earth?"

"I hope not," he said. "How very dull that would be. You and I are anything but dull."

"What is this thing we call love? Is it something nebulous? Is it just cirrus clouds on a sunshiny day?" I asked.

"It's sunrises and sunsets," he answered, "an old loom, a blanket on the beach, a B & B on an island, karaoke, dancing with you, singing *Lara's Theme*." He pretended to hold a mic. "Shall I sing to you? It's a stack of the best Belgium waffles in all of Scandinavia. My dear, it is you. Fiza, you are my love."

"I'll try to remember all those things. I certainly won't forget who spoke of them. I'm going to pack light. Maybe, your words are all I need."

We kissed. Each kiss seemed to take on special meaning. A promise of forever now that we were engaged. Fear that there wouldn't be many more before I left. Desperation of not knowing what the future held.

"Let's stand here till we become stone," he whispered into my hair. "Rodin's Kiss Statue stuck in this strait-laced street in Ornskoldsvik."

Scene Twenty-Nine
A Drive Too Short.

We were in the car, ready to go to the airport when Mom and Dad drove up. David stayed in the car, and I got out to meet them. Not wanting to make a long-drawn-out teary scene, I'm sure they had been parked just down the street, waiting for this moment. "Oh," Mom said, "I'm glad we caught you. We've come to wave you off. Dad has an envelope to give you."

"Don't open it until you are on the plane," Dad said, giving it to me. "A quick hug and you must get on your way." We had a three-person hug. "Okay, scoot, Fiza. You don't want to miss your plane," Dad added. When I was getting in the car, he bent down and said to David, "Come by the house for dinner when you get back. We'll eat whenever you come."

"Thanks," David said. He started the car, and we drove off.

"They meant it when they said they had come to wave us off," I said, when we were turning the corner and I caught sight of them. "They're still waving."

We took the same route to the airport that I took when I first came to Ornskoldsvik. Only now it was in reverse. I was going back. When I came, I remember thinking how clean everything looked. Over time, things probably haven't changed, but the brightly painted houses no longer astonished me. Dad often reminded me that my first comment on our way in from the airport, nearly twenty years ago, was, "What have they done with all the bumps?" Trying to have the reality sink in, of where I was going, I tried to imagine dust-colored buildings and bumps in the road. In this beautiful city, that kind of projection is impossible, so

I asked David, "Besides work, Prince, and Gertrude, what will you do when I'm away?"

"I want to play the guitar and write lyrics. I'll busy myself with jazz, musical notes, guitar riffs, and take my scotch lightly."

David's voice took on a certain tone when he spoke of music, and I heard yearning in his voice. I said, "I really hope you make time to do that. And David, you must keep going to the karaoke bar."

"I'll sing *Lara's Theme* and dedicate it to my love who is overseas."

"I'll be listening."

"When I first got off of skid row, I took art therapy. I could lose myself for hours trying to express something. Perhaps I'll pick up the brush again. I'll paint you," he said.

"How will you paint me?" I asked. "How do you see me?"

"Naked, of course." He smirked.

"No, seriously, David. What do you see?"

"A simple outline." He drew a female figure in the air with one hand. He put both hands on the wheel and concentrated on driving, but I sensed he was giving thought to his painting. He added, "Intricate details. Yes, there must be intricate details... the fullness of the bust, the curve of the back, the tilt of the head."

He enjoyed being dramatic, flinging his imaginary brush over the curvatures with exaggerated strokes. He had me in stitches of laughter. "Don't laugh," he admonished, in fun. "This is serious stuff. Just wait until the next straight stretch and I'll tell you the real serious stuff."

"I can hardly wait," I said.

"Now," he said, "I want to be serious. I see you as complex and complicated. If I ever paint you, I will try to have it show those most admirable qualities."

"Thank you, David. That's kind of you. Do you think you'll write to me, share your lyrics? I'm told that the snail mail in Africa is like a sloth stuck in the bottom of the honey jar, but eventually it gets through. Of course, there's the internet, but it's a far cry from what Sweden has. Apparently, there are pockets where it's okay, but even in those places, it can be unreliable. I would love to get a real letter I can hold and read as often as I need to."

He took my hand, "Of course I'll write. I'm sure you'll find yourself buzzing around in my lyrics."

"I'll write you, often. My words might not be lyrical, but they'll be from my heart."

"Thank you, Fiza. I'll be waiting for them."

Scene Thirty
Goodbye

W e were exchanging gifts of words. Words we would carry, treasure. Words that would get us through rough times. Words that we would never forget. Magical words that we could depend on to do magical things.

"I'll never forget our first dance. Every time you flung me away from you, you brought me back closer. It was on that date that I knew you were the man I wanted to spend the rest of my life with. You move so fluently. When I'm away, don't stand still. I want to think of you and Prince running along the seashore."

"I don't remember the dance as much as I remember the way you looked at me. It made me tremble, made me forget everything else but you. I'll do my best to do what you ask."

"Sing and send your words on the winds, over the seas, to me."

"Fiza, darling, with all my being I love you. I'll wait forever for you."

I stole those words and the warm loving look in his eyes, and put them in my heart for safe keeping. *One day I might need them.*

We kissed for a long time, not wanting to part, expressing where our words had failed. But I couldn't let all the kisses and words keep me here.

He reached into his pocket and took out a small object. He held it in his opened palm, and it caught the light. It was half of the heart-shaped lapis lazuli crystal. He clipped it onto my gold neck chain that he had given me on our last dinner date. We had decided that in South Sudan that I should wear my valuables inconspicuously, hence my engagement ring and now my half heart were around my neck, under my clothing. At that dinner, he had the waiter take a picture of us. I carry a wallet-size of it.

"With love," he whispered.

"Thank you, David. I'll cherish it." I shook like a leaf and my eyes stung, so before I broke down, I stepped away and said, "Don't worry, David. I'm like a weed. No matter how many times I get plucked, I grow back even taller."

I walked to the gate, then looked back and mouthed, "I love you."

I think he replied, "Forever."

Part Two
South Sudan

Scene Thirty-One
Letters — Mom and Dad

On the plane, I opened the envelope that Dad had given me at the car when he said goodbye.

Fiza don't go with the expectation that a thousand lights will suddenly go on and you will be enlightened and live happily ever after. That only happens in fairy tales. In real life it, most often, takes time and reflection before you can see the small nuances that make the biggest differences in our lives. Journey well. With Love, Dad.

My dear Fiza, the substance of who you are, more than likely, will be tested. Approach yourself tenderly with a candle of compassion. If you get only a glimpse of what you are looking for, be grateful. Like Dad says these things take time and patience. You might not realize, until you get back, that this journey was the right choice. I want you to know I have a very positive feeling that everything will be perfect. Remember: The sun in Africa is not black. Give yourself and your thoughts plenty of sunshine. I wait for your safe return with a heart filled with love, Mom.

I had a lot of time on the long flights to think. *Who am I, now that I am separated from everything that made up my life—my family of origin, my adopted family, the man I love, my friends, especially my fellow workers at The Store, my turret, my things that hold meaning for me?*

Am I disappearing from that life? Is it my destiny to make a new one?

I wrestled with my hyphenated identity—Sudanese-Swedish. *Will I erase one of them? Which one?*

Definitions of the word home wandered through the life-pages in my mind. *Will it be where my heart is? And where will that be?*

A collection of letters.

Dear Mom and Dad,

Like I told you on the phone—I have safely arrived.

On the drive from the airport, I opened the window to breathe in the evening air. It was warm and pungent—not Swedish air. *I must be here*, I thought. *I must be in Africa.*

The road, filled with potholes, also told me I wasn't in Sweden. We bypassed Juda. "We always take the safe route," the driver explained. *Whatever that means.* This detour made the ride to the hospital even longer than expected. My thoughts wandered. *The geographical roulette wheel had me born in Africa at a difficult time. By the grace of God, or chance, call it what I will, I was taken to a stable country and given the opportunity to thrive. What the Hell am I doing back here?* Although I had convinced myself that I needed to come here, I am still filled with misgivings and, I must admit, fear.

On a happier note, I must tell you something that in a million years you'll never believe.

As promised, the hospital has housed me. I share a house in the married quarters section with a young female doctor from the Netherlands. This is the part that is unbelievable. It's the house we lived in. The house that has Ellie's tree in the backyard. How miraculous is that? Your bedroom now has two single beds instead of that monster-sized bed that took up most of the space. The bathroom has been enlarged by taking half of Ellie's room. The other half is now a closet. The space in the sitting area, that you had made for me, now has a two-seater chesterfield. Even with these changes, I remember where our pictures hung, and I can still watch the passersby from the kitchen window. Sometimes, it makes me think that I never left. I wonder if you left, and I stayed. Because I'm back in the same midwifery ward it only doubles those strange feelings.

Dad, through the echo of time, I hear the words you spoke to me that night when you asked me to come with you to Sweden. I shudder to think what my life would have been like had I not gone with you. With all my heart, I'm thankful for the life you and Mom have given me. Because of you, I had an involved happy teen life, supported college days, and then the incredible chance to oversee The Store. I love you both to the moon.

You helped me develop my personality. As you say, Dad, Fiza doesn't tiptoe through the tulips; she stomps on them. And you Mom, Fiza has an opinion; and she's not shy about sharing it. And Mom, I love what Aunt Aida, says about me. Fiza is as soft as afternoon showers, but don't retire your umbrellas. If push comes to shove, she can be a raging thunderstorm. Although she isn't related, I call her Aunt Aida[12] out of respect and because she nurtured me, with love, in South Sudan and since she returned. Every time I've had a chance to visit with her, I came away with a strange feeling, a stirring in my stomach, a yearning that I never understood. I now wonder if she was a big part of my decision to come here.

You all molded me. None of you ever tolerated my innate tendency to become invisible.

I know you understand that my coming back in no way rejects all that but was necessary for me to feel settled in my life. I feel certain, unless fate intervenes, I'll come home to Sweden and will be happy.

Now, let me tell you about Ellie's Tree. It's taller than the house and is in glorious full bloom. We had a shower earlier today and the tree's fragrance still clings to the air. After the rain, the sky quickly became blue again, and I felt the sun's warmth as I hung clothes out to dry. I wondered if that's the same clothesline that you put up, Dad? I wish Ellie's tree could tell me all the stories she has of when we all lived here and the ones she's collected since we left.

My skin is already sun kissed.

I'll tell you more about the hospital when I've been there a while. Everyone is so welcoming. They make me feel comfortable.

I'll keep in touch. Would love letters from home. I send all my love. Xoxoxo **F.**

---

[12] Marlene F Cheng, *The Madam's Friend*, book four in the Love is Forever series. You can read the story, in this book, of Tijay and Aida, soulmates, pen pals, medical student classmates, doctors in South Sudan and their lives after returning to Europe.

Dear Mom and Dad,

As promised, I want to tell you about the hospital.

First, the hospital has put up a beautiful plaque. It is visible for everyone to see in the reception area:

IN APPRECIATION OF DOCTORS Z AND TIJAY'S DEVOTION AND FOR THEIR ANNUAL DONATIONS

When someone catches me reading it for the zillionth time, I proudly let them know you are my parents.

Your contact here is full of praise for the both of you. He's taken me under his wing. He's very helpful; he looks out for me. I'm saving a big hug for him when I leave.

And the Midwife Ward.

It's the young ones who were here with me before, that have become the Heads. They remember me.

I appreciate their humility, their caring, and their intelligence.

I've learned so much about delivering babies, naturally, and they are eager to learn what they call, my sterile ways.

The Chief Head's motto is selflessness. She joins all our hearts and hands in a cooperative twine and stokes the fires within us. I'll never forget what she said to me, "Fiza, you have a natural way about you. You care for people. It shows when you are handling patients and when you, without hesitation, help your peers." I carry her words and try my best to be worthy of them. I feel like I'm inside a circle of trust. The longing in my soul, to belong, is beginning to ease.

I think you know, that in Sweden, I was sometimes embarrassed to be black. But I gladly gave up who I was to fit in and be successful. Recently, as I've been questioning everything about my life, I've come to realize, by concentrating on fitting in, I lost something. Being in the ward, with such wonderful Sudanese women, points out my lost origin. I've begun to feel a responsibility to understand and own what it means to be Sudanese. Using the language has been my bridge. I practice saying with pride that I'm Sudanese. With open arms, I'm embracing all that might mean. In Sweden, my roots were there, and my branches reached out to

Africa. Now that I'm here, I wonder if I'll reclaim my African roots and have branches that reach out to Sweden.

When I was discussing this with the Chief Head, she said, "We know you have good intentions. We love having you here with us, but maybe you'll have a better life in Sweden. No matter how loudly you sing, you'll never be heard over the chaos of this country's madness."

I told her, "I understand. I know you want what's best for me. After I've been to my village, I'll decide."

The hospital, the midwife ward, my place, Ellie's tree, South Sudan, Africa. Maybe I've claimed a homecoming to this place. Then again, perhaps I'm seeing through nostalgic eyes and am overly sentimental. Over time, I may realize that my birthplace is great for a visit, but Sweden is where I want to live. I send my love. **F.**

Dear Mom and Dad,

I'm not my bubbly self today. I've become quiet, but my mind's a mess. I'm beginning to have doubts, questioning why I'm here. I'm putting my thoughts on paper for you. Perhaps you can advise.

The hospital still has the Social Club where staff members hang out when off duty. The ice box is kept stocked with cold drinks and one can order coffee or tea and finger food from the hospital kitchen. I go as often as I can, as it's at the Club where I'm beginning to get a better understanding of South Sudan. When I asked why the place was always busy, even on the weekends, a young doctor— he was probably still in diapers when you were here— told me, "We used to go into town to a restaurant, to celebrate someone's promotion or a birthday, but we don't anymore. You never know, with all the unrest, when you might come under crossfire. No one wishes to be out of the hospital compound, especially after dark."

I realize that I haven't returned to the South Sudan of the happy stories you told me as a child. Of course, there were cautionary tales, but the South Sudan today is even more chaotic and dangerous than the one you fled almost twenty years ago. That place from twenty years ago is now pure fantasy. I wonder if young lovers, today, would feel free to go canoeing on the river. I cherish those stories about the two of you. And I remember stories of you going freely back and forth to the university to teach and joining vaccination campaigns to rid the country of polio. Racism, shade-ism, is now so rampant that people think twice about going into the community. Fighting breaks out constantly, leaving no area of the country at peace. This chaos limits many socioeconomic activities and makes me wonder about the future of the country.

I read *South Sudan* by Hilde F. Johnson. She talks about this, but I didn't feel the impact of her words like I do now, being here.

Most often, everything here is too much for me. The conditions. The hospital is underfunded and there is always a lack of supplies. No antibiotics. No fortified formula for starving children. The supply-chain is constantly interrupted due to insurrections and the government's priority is funding the military. The everyday people, who are trying to feed their families and live in peace, get the sharpest edge of the sword in all this. It breaks my heart to see the lineups outside the hospital gates of people trying to get care, and in many cases the patients are released, far too early, to make room. The wards are already filled beyond capacity, with some patients sleeping on the floor. I'm told that this chaos has gone on for generations, but a senior staff member told me, "I've never seen it as bad as it is now." When will it ever stop? It rips me open. I cry for these people.

Yet even though the people are trying to keep their heads above water, it's marvelous how they are each other's life jackets. It's doesn't matter how rough the waters get; they cling to hope. They buoy each other with kindness. They drown one another in love. Food isn't hoarded; it's shared right down to the last crumb. Your friend, Nazrin, who I brought the gifts for, took me to her house. Let me say that the choice of jewelry, as gifts, was perfect. When I gave them to her, Nazrin said, "Tijay has a big heart. She knows I can take these to the market and get a good price. She has put food on our table. I've never had a better friend. After all these years, we think of each other." She still lives in the same tiny house with the basics of basic. It has the lean-to where she houses the two old helpers and an additional young one, supporting them by working at the hospital when she should be retired. They keep a small vegetable garden. When

Nazrin comes to the hospital, she leaves packets of vegetable stew, wrapped in big leaves, outside the gates for people begging for food.

I understand, Dad, how terribly torn you must have been when you were deciding whether to leave your country. I honestly believe you made the right decision.

I feel like an emigrant in my own country. South Sudan is indifferent to me. When I stand still, even the winds, without interruption, blow right through me. And where is the blame? I was the one who abandoned her. And now, I'm beginning to think I'll do it again.

Should I take the positives, all the reawakened Sudanese parts of me, and mold them in my hands, like potter's clay, to form past memories of my village and the terrorist camp? I could mold them into any shape that pleases me. Shapes I can live with. Should I forget trying to uncover **the truth** about my past, live in fantasy, and flee—come home to Sweden?

You tell me that when I set my mind to something that I always see it through. Will I have failed if I come home?

I'm beginning to think that South Sudan has been abandoned by God. Is it so wrong to want to come home and live with my family's and David's love?

The driver is leaving for town, so I must give this to him to post. The driver no longer takes the hospital van but drives the ambulance with a big red cross painted on it, and he never goes after dark.

I'll go to the ward. Perhaps the women and babies will lift my spirits.

I'll keep in touch—let you know my plans.

All my love,

F.

Dear Mom and Dad,

I might have left you worrying, so I must send off another letter.

This evening when I came back from the ward, I was up. There was a warm golden sunset, and the crickets were out in abundance, as you must remember them. Later, I watched a thousand shooting stars burn across the sky. They made me think that Grampa Y was telling me that everything would be alright. I hung my heart next to the moon for him.

I must let you know that I'm safe. The hospital compound is surrounded with a twelve-foot wall that has barbed wire rolls on top. Armed gentry walk the outside of the wall 24/7, and I often see them on the grounds.

Please don't worry,

Love, **F.**

Our Dear Fiza,

Mom and I cannot advise you. We can only tell you what we think. We trust that you will weigh the pros and cons and make wise decisions.

You're right, Fiza. It was very difficult for me to leave my country. Your being there stirs up so many thoughts of the past. In medical school, we were young and full of ambition. We wanted to change the world, our country, and medicine, but at every turn we became discouraged and were forced to let the rain wash away what we could not change. Even though I made the right decision by coming to Sweden, I sometimes feel a terrible homesickness for my birthland. Remember all the good things to bring home and share with me.

Thank you for the letter that came so quickly after the one that had us worried. It was a relief to hear that the hospital compound is fenced and patrolled. How difficult it is for us to imagine that. Don't even think about going to Kuda[13] to pay respect over my parents' graves. Mom wanted you to see the Kuda church, where we were married, but she urges you not to go.

It is my dream to go to Kuda and replace the grey, wooden, weathered crosses that mark my parents' graves with something more permanent— stone perhaps and a carving or plaque that reads:

Mother and Father
"Unfurl your wild wings and fly.

---

[13] Marlene Cheng, *The Madam's Friend*. Read about Kuda, Z. and Tijay's wedding and about Tijay's father in this book.

We'll meet on the other side of the moon."
Your loving son,
Z.

And your mom would like to put a metal bench nearby with a plaque that reads:

In memory of my father—Oriole.
Your loving daughter,
Tijay.

She would like it to be a place for people to rest and ponder.

As far as going to your village is concerned, maybe it would be wise not to go. Mom and I feel that you should rethink that.

We would like nothing more than for you to have the driver take you, as soon as possible, in daylight, to the airport.

You must keep in touch. If you decide to go to your village, please phone and let us know. I realize how unreliable the phones can be, but letters take too long. You might be on your way before we even know. And getting a letter to us from the village might be difficult.

We are all fine here. David comes by to keep us up to date on Gertrude, and we share our concerns about you.

Your siblings ask constantly if we have heard anything. We try hard not to let them hear our worries. Sister Ellie was so excited when we told her that you were staying in the same place where we lived.

We send our love on a wing and a prayer, and hope you feel it.
Dad.

Our Dearest Fiza,

How wonderful to hear your voice and to wish you a Merry Christmas. Through all the echoing on the phone, we hope you felt how sincere our wishes are for you. We hold all positive thoughts that you'll have a successful, happy New Year. You've been gone almost three months and it feels like an eternity. We really appreciate your letters. Keep them coming.

With all our love,
Dad and Mom.

Our Dearest Fiza,

David and I keep the turret in good condition. We worry that we might be overwatering the plants. I found a love note in the black pansies. It was meant, I'm sure, for David to find, so I watered the plant and repotted the love note.

David goes to the turret to play his guitar and write music. He opens the window so people can hear the music and not think the turret is vacated. He says the vibrations keep the dust from settling.

Every now and then, I go to The Store to say hi. Sue is doing a good job. She tells me they have a new design to feature in the Spring Collection. I'm to keep it a secret. Sue wants your curiosity to entice you to come home.

I wander over to Gertrude's Place to have a chat with David. The other day, he oiled every part of Gertrude that moves. It takes him the better part of a day. He froths milk and makes me coffee, and has Prince demonstrate his latest learned command. My, that dog is clever. I'm glad David has Prince, Gertrude, and his guitar. I can tell he's lonely. He tells me how much he misses you.

He has framed and hung a large picture of the two of you on the wall by Gertrude. It's lovely. It must have been taken just before you left; you're wearing your engagement ring on a chain around your neck.

Gramma Tree keeps busy and is in good health. Because we have all this extra space, and we think it's nonsense to keep up two places, she has moved in with us. She's writing her memoir, *The Place of Memories*. When we told her that you won't be going to Kuda, she was disappointed. It has been officially confirmed that Kuda was her husband's— my father's— home village. She wanted you to go to the city hall and see his entry in the records.

That's it for now. Please keep in touch. We want to hear the truth of how you are and what you plan but be as gentle as you can because your dad worries so. He paces, muttering to himself.

He wants to see you home. And so do we all.

You left on September 30th and it's now coming spring—a long time for us to be without you.

Sending our love, Mom.

My Dear Fiza,

On one of my visits to Gertrude's Place, David showed me how well Gertrude is shaping up. He asked me not to tell you, so I won't. He wants it to be a surprise. We all assume that you'll soon discover what you are looking for and will come home.

We got to talking. He said that you had told him your story. You remembered going up the path, out of your village with a man, but you haven't told him anything beyond that. He wanted to know how you came to be adopted and how you ended up in Sweden. So, I told him.[14] He was most interested and asked many questions.

I hope you don't mind that I filled in your story for him.

Oh yes, I almost forgot. Huong's punch needled and embroidery handbags and cushions are selling like hotcakes. She now holds night classes at The Store where she teaches young people visible mending. I think it's becoming a trend. I've spotted torn jeans with visible mending all around town. My, but people are creative. I saw tigers running across one person's knees.

I don't have any further news. I just wanted to let you know how The Store is doing and what I've told David.

Dad and I send our love. In case you ever wonder, we want you to know that you are as much our child as the other children. We love you all, to the moon.

Mom.

Mom and Dad,

Last night in the howling winds, the house shook. I thought it might crumble. It scared me half to death. I made up my mind. I was going home.

I couldn't sleep, so I thought about home and what you had written about Huong. Tell her there's embroidery done in Paris on a manually

---

[14] Marlene F Cheng, *The Madam's Friend, Book Four in the Love is Forever Series.* Fiza's story is included in this book.

operated machine from the early 19th century. She needs a holiday. Encourage her to go to Paris and have a look. The names Marseille and Cornely come to mind.

Today, there was a downpour. The raindrops bounced a foot high off the barren ground, sending dust flying. It only lasted a few minutes, and the after smell was Heavenly—sweet, good earth. Then, a double rainbow bent down from the sky and landed in the copse over on the hill.

I changed my mind. I'm going to my village. It should take a few days to prepare. I'll phone you the day before I leave.

I didn't get this to the post. I'm on my way, so will mail it in town. How good it was to hear your voices.

The girls from the ward pinned flowers in my hair for good luck and it seemed like the entire hospital staff came out to wave me off.

I'm on my way. I'm on my way.

As soon as I'm able, I'll get word to you. Please don't worry. You know me, I'll take every precaution.

The stars are aligned in my favor. I feel extremely positive and excited. My inner spark is threatening to burst into flames.

Sending my love,

F.

Scene Thirty-Two
Letters — David

I remember the day this letter arrived. No letter had come from David in two weeks, and I was terribly homesick. The hospital driver, who brings the mail, was going mad with my asking if I had any. Then today, he came to the ward and said, "Missy, you have mail."

"Thank you. Thank you," I said. I could tell from the neat printing it was from David and I tucked it under my scrubs next to my heart. I would wait until after my shift and find someplace private to open it. On the path home, I stepped aside and found a rock to sit on. I read:

My Dear Fiza,

That's all I needed. The flood gates opened, and the tears ran freely. All the waiting. The homesickness. I clutched the letter to me. The late-day, sweet scent of the poinciana bushes reminded me that I was in Africa and David was miles away. *What am I doing here? Am I out-of-my-mind? When did I last tell him that I loved him?*

A pair of mourning doves regularly share my coffee break. I'm beginning to know their habits. One eats while the other stands watch, high up in a neighboring tree. It takes me back to my tour of duty in Afghanistan when having your buddy's back was a given. Are you and I like that? Taking turns watching out for each other?

Oh, David, how I wish I were there with you. I want to watch out for you. I want you to watch out for me. How can that happen when we are so far apart? Have I done the wrong thing by coming here?

I've been writing lyrics about you. I've labelled them, "Fiza's Song." You are the most difficult song I've ever written. When I've

finished working on the guitar arrangement and am satisfied, I'll send the words to you.

How sweet. Or maybe, not. What might he say about me?

Sue and I keep the red lily's soil wet. She's done research and discovered that the plant might do well with some mushroom manure. Whatever that is? "My gosh, Sue, this species survived God knows how many years in the wild. We mustn't smother it with too much kindness," I remind her. None-the-less, I've found that smelly stuff, and I rake it in the soil, sparingly. I do hope I haven't killed it.

Those words made me smile. I could imagine the two of them fussing over my plant. Both would be devastated if they couldn't keep it alive for me. I read his mushy salutation, folded his letter, and put it in my pocket. On the rest of my walk home, I couldn't help reciting Gilbert &Sullivan's:

> "Oh joy, Oh rapture unforeseen,
> The clouded sky is now serene."

Dearest David,

I like your version of me. I'm banking on all that courage you say I have, hoping it'll see me through this.

You're always here with me when I write. I feel your breeze blowing through my pen. A memory whiff of Paco Rabanne—evergreen with a dash of lemon. Oh! How I do miss it.

Thanks for the red lily report. Has it survived your kindness?

This letter came near the beginning of November. I had been here just over a month. It's the first letter where David opened about missing me. I've read this one so many times and cried over it so often that the words are getting blurry. It made me realize that I'm not the only one who I've made lonely, and I feel sorry for what I'm putting David through.

My Love,

Today, for the first time, I saw a red bird. Might it be a cardinal? It sang so sweetly. I took its song to be a message from

you. It sang, "Listen, listen, listen." Fiza, I'm listening, but no letter has come for quite a few days.

I'm so sorry, David. This is no excuse, but I'm exhausted after a shift on the ward, and I go to the social club to try and learn about the situation here. I'll try and write, if only a few lines, more often.

This is a heart song from the lovesick.

I love you. I want you. I need you.

Oh God, David. Those words make me want to fly to you. I want to hold you and tell you how much I love you. How can I say, never let me go, when I'm the one that insisted on coming here?

How much longer must I wait?

Now, you've really got to me. I wish I could say, I'm coming, but I really don't know. I'm still questioning if coming here has been all wrong.

Some days I'm fine. Others, not.

It's difficult to get out of my own way, wandering from this to that.

I'm so sorry. I must ask Mom and Dad to take him for a night out at the Karaoke Café. Maybe, that'll give him a lift.

I just want you here, safe.

I have no one to be opinionated with, no one to tell me stories about mugs, about scent, about lost looms in Welsh pastures, or was that Irish fields? I've forgotten. Please come and refresh me.

There's one yellow rose clinging to your rose bush. It waits for you.

How sweet of you, David, to turn your words away from your loneliness and give me a taste of home that I need. I must ask if it's too late to press the last rose of summer.

I've built a frame around the red lily. I'll wrap it if it gets too cold.

And one of the huge bobbins that sits at the entrance to The Store has cracked open. I've brought it in, clued it, and now have it tied securely with ropes. I do hope I've rescued it, as I know how much you like them.

How thoughtful, David. When you do things like that, it pleases me so. It makes my heart sing.

My Dearest,

I long for the taste of your frothy coffee on my lips.

I think of standing at the window in my turret and looking down to the twilit sea. Lines from Percy Bysshe Shelley's *Hymn to Intellectual Beauty* come to me.

> "Like aught that for its grace may be
> Dear, and yet dearer for its mystery."

I think about why I came here in the first place. Am I willing to forget what abuse might have happened to me that causes me to panic when we wish to make love? I wonder if I've seen enough, and I will no longer panic.

I need to do some serious soul-searching.

Should I forget everything and come home?

Do I really want to rip open old forgotten wounds?

I say all this, to let you know I'm at an impasse. Shall I come home, or should I go on?

I'll let you know as soon as I've got it figured out.

P.S. How many years did you tell Sue that red lilies survived in the wild? Now look who is domesticating my plant. I love you for taking care of it. My dear, sweet, bobbin savior.

My Darling Fiza,

Your thoughts are loud, Fiza. I can even hear the words that you are not saying.

The shoreline looks desolate without you, your driftwood, lonely.

Prince and I sent loving thoughts to you on invisible winds.

We trust your sensitive soul embraced them.

And I hummed a vibration of love songs to the stars.

Did you hear them?

I cherish your letters and can't wait to read them out loud to you. One day soon, I hope.

Perchance, to ease your contractions when you're giving birth to our first child. How's that for magical thinking? Or should I say wishful?

You see, Fiza, I listened when you said your dream was to love someone and to be loved, to have a house with a yard where children could play.

In the meantime, I've been adjusting some of the heddles. The shuttle flies off if it comes to an impasse. I've become adept at escaping a blow to the head. I've read that most contemporary factories have eliminated the shuttle on their looms. This makes production quicker. Would you consider doing that?

Love,

David, your songs are in my soul, but I miss the beautiful voice that sang them.

I wish you were here. I wish you were here.

It's late. My eyes are growing dim, but then a thought of you comes and they brighten, and my pen wants to scribble my most heartfelt endearments.

I love you to the moon.

Your wishful thinking makes me feel all warm and cozy.

More than anything in the whole wide world, I want you and me to be in that house with the backyard and the apple tree. It's that dream that keeps me thinking that I do need to go to my village.

As far as the shuttle goes—David, it's important to me to have authentic heirloom blankets. They must have a true selvedge. This means that they won't need any further finishing to prevent unravelling. Therefore, Gertrude needs her shuttle and pick heads. I can imagine your shuttle dance, and it makes me smile. Should I send a helmet?

Dearest Fiza,

Sometimes, when I'm here at night in your turret, I see shadows of the night owl as she flies past the windows. When I open the panes, I hear her hoot, hoot—a lovely night song. I should invite her in to sing backup.

It is my wish that my music will enchant you. It expresses my feelings.

My Dear David,

I'm dying to taste the squeeze of your lemon tarts. My baker extraordinaire.

Are my black pansies blooming? Check that the soil is damp.

Fiza. I'm beside myself with awe.

You'll never in a million years guess what happened.

A small package came to my engineering office.

Inside was a note: I put your business card in my catch-all drawer. But something about it kept my mind uneasy. I couldn't understand why. One day I happened on this, and a light went on. I remembered that it had come off from the guitar you bought. I checked. David Jones. Was it possible, I wondered? So, I'm sending it to you. Let me know if my hunch is right. Lars, from the music shop on the Island.

As you might guess, it was the plaque that my high school had attached to the guitar, when it was presented to me. I looked closely, and the darker rectangle is still visible on the back of the guitar I bought from Lars.

I really thought I had bought my own guitar. And I was right.

I wish it could talk. I would love to hear its travels from a pawn shop in Mississippi to a music store on an isolated island in Sweden.

I'm going back to the Islands. I want to know how it got to Lar's music store.

Isn't that the most incredible thing?

David.

I'm to the moon happy for you.

I can't wait to hear the entire saga.

Are you sure that the shuttle didn't hit you and blow your mind into a wishful-thinking fantasy?

This letter came after I had made up my mind that I was, without any doubts, going to my village.

Fiza, my lovely,

Ever since I met you, I've changed with each season. Just as a reminder, I first walked into The Store in February and now it's nearing the middle of April the following year. So, I've been through all the seasons with you. I think I'm getting closer to the man I want to be. I'm proud to say, even with missing you, I haven't had an episode of depression. I keep to my regular appointments with the psychiatrist, and spend wonderful times with Mr. and Mrs. Doc. I have your letters and your parents support to thank. And the staff at The Store invite me for coffee or drop by to chat when I'm working on Gertie. And music has been my healer, my saving grace. It lifts me.

I'm so happy for you, David. How wonderful. This gives me courage to face up to my past. It makes me willing to do anything for our future happiness. You've done your best, and I'm proud of you. I want you to be proud of me.

The air is chilly here, but thoughts of you are all the warmth I need. I think about your rum raisin eyes, your coal-black curly hair. I love how strands escape, no matter how hard you try to keep it neat in a bun. And I miss the lavender smell of it. And I miss you. And I miss you. And I miss you. Oh! How I miss you so much.

And I miss you. I think of your sparkling eyes and your captivating grin when you are being playful. I love how you move so gracefully when you run. And when you dance! I can hardly wait to dance again, with you.

For days I've watched a spider spinning. Her chains glisten from ceiling to light fixture, to the top of the cupboards. Such

artistry. I don't know how to protect her from the cleaner's swipe. It makes me feel sad. Just like I feel sad knowing I'm not there to protect you. Sad and helpless.

Please don't feel sad. We spoke, many times, about how this is something I must do on my own. Once I get into the bush on the trail, I think it'll be safer than being in the town of Juda, with all the upheaval.

Prince and I went to the beach. I wrote you a love note on the waning moon. I hope you read it before the moon tipped it out. In case you didn't catch it, this is what it said:

A Secret Surprise.

I couldn't imagine what his surprise might be. As soon as I read his letter, I wrote back to him, then ran to catch the driver before he left to go to the post office.

David,

You can't do this to me. Please don't keep your surprise secret. Has Gertrude started to weave? Is that it?

Please respond immediately, as I'm leaving soon to go to the village. I want to take your letter next to my heart. I want to carry your soul in my pocket and tuck your heart under my pillow each night.

Don't disappoint. Please tell me your secret.

David,

Your letter didn't come.

I'm despondent.

I'm at the post office. I would wait, but the postmaster says that he doesn't expect any more mail for days.

I'm on my way to my village.

I'll get word to you as soon as I'm able.

I love you. I love you. I love you.

David, I love you.

I'll come back, so you can finish writing our lyrics.

Yours forever, Fiza.

On the drive into Juda, I thought of the life at the hospital that I might have left, for good. The women in the Midwifery Ward constantly asked me to tell them stories about winter in Sweden. They went wide-eyed at the wonder of a white world. Thinking about those stories took my mind from nefarious thoughts and it helped to pass the time driving over the rickety road. So, for fun, I'll include a couple of those stories here.

One winter night I was outside, taking in the beauty of the knee-deep snow. A full moon glimmered over the banks. It was crisp cold. From the snow-covered pine tree by The Store, came the most thrilling sound. A night owl sang to me.

"Sing the song of the night owl," they insisted. I did my best hooting. After that, whenever we were dancing and singing, celebrating a new birth, hoot hoot, was always added.

Another time, when I was visiting in the North of Sweden, my friends took me outside to witness lights of every colour flashing across the sky. The winds blew the lights closer and closer, mesmerizing me. This display is called The Northern Lights. To add to the amazing show, several white wolves howled.

"Howl like a wolf," they requested.

"Owooooo." Owooooo became the salutation to all our celebrations.

I remember saying to those wide-eyed women, "Just imagine, this African girl privileged with those sights and sounds."

And I would boast how I could identify the different noises snow makes.

"The snow makes different noises?" they would ask.

"Depending on the temperature, there's a wet crunching and an ice crystal crushing sound. On freezing nights, when there were no clouds, snowflakes layer on top of each other and stick to bare tree branches and telephone wires, creating a ghost-like magical scene. It's called *hoarfrost*."

"Unbelievable," they would gasp in wonder. "It's scary," they would say, feigning a shiver.

The ride had me thinking about when I first came to the hospital. There are sixty different languages spoken in Sudan. Many distinct dialects were represented on the midwifery ward. The women's tongues rolled out words as if they were singing. I heard the notes and felt their meaning before I understood what was said. Being with them everyday and with great encouragement, I soon became surprisingly fluent in what is loosely referred to as Juba Arabic, and I had practise in Dinka, or a version of it. Dinka was close to the dialect that was spoken in my village, Dad had informed me.

Dinka fit my mind better than my English. This was the language that connected me by birthright and heritage to my native place. It gave me wonder how much, of South Sudan and what had happened here, had seeped into me during my young awakening years. What language had I stored those memories in?

Scene Thirty-Three
In the Bush

The hospital driver took me into Juda. On my way to the hospital, when I first arrived, we had by-passed the town. In all the months that I'd been here, I had never left the hospital compound other than to walk to Nazrin's, which was a quarter of a mile away. Juda was much smaller than I had imagined. The mostly one-story buildings *looked* drag and dingy. Paint was non-existent or pealing. The pot-holed main street looked to be the only one that was paved. As far as I could make out, the side streets were narrow dirt pathways. I suppose, subconsciously, I was comparing it to Ornskoldsvik with its spic and span, brightly colored houses, and I wasn't impressed. We went to the post office, a shack that was much in need of repair. "Mind the second step," the driver warned. "The boards are warped, and you can trip." The calendar, the lone decoration on the wall, showed April fifteen. That date will always stick with me. Six and a half months after coming to South Sudan, I was, after many deliberations, going to my village. The driver took me to the head of the trail. "Good luck, missy. Go to the Civic Building and phone the hospital when you need a ride back. Take care."

There was a wooden marker, with a number on it, pounded into the ground. I imagined that it identified the trail, as a few different trails led to villages that surrounded Juda. I didn't need its assistance. Immediately, I recognized an ancient banyan tree, with hundreds of hanging branches. It gave off an odour of wet mud that stirred some forgotten memory. And across the street was the Civic Building where Dad had taken me to get my adoption papers. Before I left Sweden, Dad had reminded me of these landmarks. "Look for the Lion's Head on the Civic Building," he told me. And indeed, The Lion's Head was there.

Here I was. Here I was at the trail I had walked up when I left my village. For a moment, I was immobile. I started to shake. My stomach felt queasy. My legs gave out. Sitting on the ground, I put my head between my knees, trying to quell the impulse to vomit. *My God, what's happening to you? Pull yourself together. What do you feel?*

I feel sick. I feel abandoned. I feel like I'm all alone in a world with a problem that's too big. I feel defeated. Not knowing what else to do, I waited. Perhaps I was hoping for a miracle. Maybe I was thinking if I waited long enough that I would wake up from this terrible nightmare and find myself in my turret in Sweden. The nausea passed. I stood up with determination and said out loud, "I feel like I'm standing at the doorway to my dreams."

Buoyed by my newfound enthusiasm, I started down the path. *It's not that bad, nothing is ever too hard, nothing is ever too much,* I encouraged myself.

Breezes drifted along the path, bringing the sweet smell of plants that I could not name but recognized by their scent. With every footstep, I was reminded of my footsteps that went in the other direction, eons ago. I could no more forget my way along this trail through these bushes than I could forget my name.

Since I've been in Africa, my gift of seeing—seeing with the eyes of my soul—has strengthened. And being in the outdoors enhanced this gift. *I'm open to whatever guidance my gift will bring.* I came by an irrigation pond and stood by the water's edge, next to a mulberry thicket, morus nigra. A mist came down from the sky, suspended over the water. An eerie feeling of being watched came to me. Shivers ran up my spine. I intuitively understood that I was getting a message. A whooshing whistle and a gentle gust blew past, lifting my hair and bending the mulberry bushes. It vanished into stillness. After being distracted by the bending of the bushes, I returned my gaze to the water. The fog figures had gone. *What was all that about? Someone wants me to know that they are watching over me.* I looked up and mouthed, "Thank you."

I studied the color of the berries. When fully ripe, they are edible. I picked some, then continued. The path wove downhill, and the brush became sparse. The landscape had become more like a plain. This was the typical picture I have when I think of Africa. The few stunned trees. The cracked earth. The dust. And the realization came that I was now where wild creatures might roam. *I must keep alert. Look for a tree that has some height and is climbable. Don't run. Play dead.* I took my wild animal spray from my backpack and carried it. The local people who worked at the hospital told me that because the path was constantly used, it was unlikely that I would see a wild animal. "Whistle, or make a lot of noise, so you don't surprise them. They are as afraid of you as you are of them," everyone said. *Constantly used? I haven't met a single soul.*

To quell my fear, I think of David. At times, I think I hear him behind me, shoes crunching leaves. My heart leaps in anticipation, as I turn to look. A ground grouse skitters across the path, wing hanging low. She's trying to lead me away from her nest. *Stop dreaming*, I tell myself. *His boots must be crunching the last of the snow in Ornskoldsvik.*

My mind reaches forward along the path, questioning. *Will anyone recognize me? Will the tree that grew by Father's tukul still be there? Will the hole in the fence still be passable? Where once these places stood, will there be nothing? Will my past be lost to me, forever? Will this entire effort be futile? Will my longing never be fulfilled?* In my mind's eye I visualized a thriving village, a warm welcoming, a much older but still capable aunt. No matter how hard I tried, I couldn't visualize the hole in the fence, probably because I had no memory of it. Visualization, of course, didn't give me the answers. I still had to see for myself.

The plain eventually gave way, and I was again among bushes. Suddenly, the fear, I was trying to suppress, grabbed me full on, and I had a panic attack not unlike what happened to me before I started down the trail. I shook uncontrollably. The root infested path made me think of snakes. I'm frightened to death of snakes. I stopped, trying to figure out how to step over all these quivering reptiles.

Then, I saw the army ants. Just a few feet in front of me, a twelve-inch scourge marched across my path. "Oh, God," I screamed, and ran in the direction I had just come. I remembered being told as a child, "Don't step over an ant march. Wait until they pass. Yell for help." *Good advice,* I think. *And who will hear me?*

I had a pressing urge to relieve myself. *What? And expose my parts to any number of creepy crawlers.* I crossed my legs and danced on the spot, hoping the urge would pass. It didn't. I took a half squat stance and quickly emptied my bladder. My pant legs got sprayed and my boots got wet. I used the minimum amount of toilet paper that I had taken from the hospital. It wasn't pure white and supreme softness that had spoiled me in Sweden; it was dark and rough, but at least it was a step up from having to use leaves. I buried the used paper.

Keeping my distance, I checked if the army ants had passed. There was not an ant in sight and the roots stopped quivering, so I continued.

My thoughts turned to what just happened. *It must be divine intervention. How does the universe know that snakes terrify me? If I had stepped on the ants, I might have been bitten to death.* I had noticed a few three-foot-tall ant hills in the distance as I walked, but I hadn't imagined that ants would cross my path. Another lesson learned. Don't make what you think are intellectual assumptions, unless backed by personal experiences. And, even then, be open to doubts.

My thoughts about divine intervention gave me security. The idea that I was being watched over and protected lifted my spirits. I drank from my water bottle and chewed on an energy bar. *I feel good.* I quickened my pace, making up for the time lost over the ant incident. My goal was to camp overnight, just outside my village, and I wanted to reach there before dark.

My positive feelings were short lived. I heard the swish of branches, the snap of twigs. Every time I stopped to look and listen, I saw nothing, and the noises stopped. My heart pounded. My breath quickened. I broke out in a cold sweat. *Was I being stalked? It can't be an animal, or it wouldn't stop, just because I hesitate.* All the horror stories I'd been told at the hospital, about maniacal people on terrorist attacks, flooded my mind. *What shade do people think I am? Grey or black? How could anyone tell?* I was covered head to toe in camouflage for protection against insect bites and the sun, and to be invisible. God forbid someone would get close enough to see my face. It was some consolation that I saw and sensed auras. I could determine whether a person is angry. I tried to erase the negative by telling myself I was on a walk in the park, that I was taking a sweet stroll down a garden lane. But it didn't work; reality won out. *It's too rough. This is all much too difficult. I can't do this anymore. The unknown is too big. The possibilities quake me. I'm scared.* I began to run, which wasn't easy with my heavy backpack of supplies. My backpack shifted, causing me to lose my balance, and I fell face down in the dirt. Although the dirt was dust, I felt like I was trapped in mud up to my neck. I couldn't move.

I have never consciously prayed, but a powerful instinct to survive flooded through me, and desperate words cried out from deep inside my heart, "Please, Guardian Angel. Please protect me." Their echo, resonating off the parched earth, watered my arid soul and lit my mind. *You can either lie here and die, to be eaten by vultures, or you can get up and go on. Did you come this far for it all to end like this?*

Indecision was the strangler. This entire journey had been an emotional roller coaster. I was exhausted to the bone. I raised my head and spat out the dust. "Oh!" I said. "The air smells like rain coming."

Iron grey clouds thundered. Lightning scorched across the sky. "A cloud burst must be close."

I stood and hurried on. As what happens so often here, the threatening storm passed, leaving not a drop of rain. I took it to be a positive sign, and scurried on, keeping my eyes focused on looking for a shelter.

Soon it was dusk, and fireflies frolicked.

I set up camp just off the fork in the path, pitching my pup tent among the bushes and setting up my one-burner, propane camp stove on a rock, far from overhanging branches. I boiled just enough water to make a cup of jasmine tea, then sat on my small ground sheet to savour my drink in its tin cup. I wanted to relax before preparing a meal.

My body was still, but my mind was racing. *What's next?* was the prominent thought. I got up and with a stick drew two lines. One across the path to my village and one across the path that led through the bush to the Terrorist's Camp. I would decide which one to erase first. By erasing it, I would be opening my passage in that direction.

What is my main purpose for *going to either?* I pondered, while eating a sparse meal prepared from a package of dried lentils and snow peas. *Am I truly going to the village to see what's become of my family's plot of land? Or do I want to face the ones that held me in disdain when I came back from The Camp as damaged goods? Do I want to show them that I am worthy of respect, that my face has value?*

I wrapped an emergency blanket—*how can this tin-foil thing be called a blanket*— around my shoulders, my hands around an after-dinner cup of hot tea. Intermittently, I dunked a cube of dried mango in my tea to soften the fruit, and sucked every drop of sweetness it offered, stretching out the few cubes I had. I sat, waiting for the sun to set.

Flashes of various shades of vermillion and yellows twisted into tints of orange. A concentration of the palest green floods patches of golden pink. Then, having gathered all of life's mysteries, the twilit sky dipped beneath the horizon. There's a Sudanese poet who believes that when a sun sets it closes everything that happened that day—all of life's mysteries— and opens us up for a new beginning with tomorrow's sunrise. If I believed that, I wouldn't have given a thought to my past. I wouldn't be here in the bush, looking for answers.

All was black and for a few moments, silent.

A bird song gave me something to think about besides my current situation. *It might be a southern red bishop. Is it a she-bird? Has her kind, over millennia, shed their colorful plumages and given them to the he-birds? Am I, a contemporary woman, trying to recover a meaningful plumage?* Her song beat in tune with my aching heart, resonating in my stumbling soul. Somehow, it rested my troubled mind. I was at peace.

The galaxies domed the earth. The sparkling stars, the delicacy of the milky way, the moon sliver, smiling, took my breath away. "Grampa," I whispered, "I can't find our star. A myriad of ancient stars keeps you from me, but the brightness of their light brings you close. I sense the pulse of your being out there in the universe, bouncing off the moon's glow, skating among the southern cross. Is that the flapping of angel's wings that I hear? Or is it, in my imagination, you humming? I have a request. Please Grampa, please. Would you tell my family that their eldest daughter has come home to pay her respects?"

A falling star flashed across the sky, carrying Grampa's words to me, "Fiza, always remember, I believe in you. When the whole world goes wrong, Grampa will still believe in you. And God willing, my love, you'll learn to believe in yourself."

His words warmed me. They gave me strength. They made me believe that I had purpose. "I'll do my best," I answered, and in that moment, I believed in the power of prayer, and knew that all was well in Heaven and Earth.

I stared into the brightness of the sky. Meteorites took me to *that terrorist camp*. A memory was sparked. I remembered such a flare in the sky that frightened all the young-boy soldiers. They thought they were being shot at by missiles.

Suddenly, I was back in that camp, lost in that place of desolation and despair.

A thinned-tailed mousebird dropped from its upside-down-hanging in the rotting timbers and whispered in my ear, "You are not the sinner. You are God's beautiful child. Leave this place, the abyss where nothingness dwells, and never, ever forget that."

A woodpecker punctuated the mousebird's words, hammering them into me.

Together, without giving me the dirty details, they made me understand the deepest depths of what went on in that cruel place. A trembling of recognitions, of things that had been hidden inside me, erupted. What was silent became sound; cracking of bones, screams of horror, gun shots. What was invisible became visible; blood, raw guts, rotting bodies. And I found pieces of me that had been completely forgotten, the child slave, the vanquished childhood, and most vividly, the ten-year-old me, crying while being raped.

One part of me realized I was convulsing on the ground, tearing my emergency blanket to shreds, trying to escape from that place. Another part of me knew I had to face this truth. A courage that I didn't know I possessed came to me.

I offered grace to those who had harmed me and pinned forgiveness on the Southern Cross. I wasn't white washing over my past. I had remembered; and now all I wanted was to forget.

"Your saving grace," the mousebird said, "will be your forgiveness. It will define your life as you move on from this dark night of your soul."

"And don't let anything or anybody gaslight you," the woodpecker added. "You have no reason to question your sanity."

The light of knowing washed over me, and I felt a fresh fullness of innocence regained. And dwelling in that fullness was love, trust, and belonging. I trusted that I could love without hesitation and belong without having to hide my dirtiness.

"Trailing clouds of glory,"[15] my precious, beautiful inner child came to me.

I held her close and rocked her, planting gentle kisses, she had never known on her face.

She fluttered like a butterfly with the joy of it.

In gratitude, we bent together, in reverence, and kissed our birth earth.

We stood and holding each other fast, we danced, Afrobeat.

Tiny dancing girl full of joy, stars for eyes. In the earthy sounds of the drums and rattles and shakers, we caught the language of our native tongue. How sweet the sound—long forgotten intonations of family, of belonging, of moving in rhythm.

We melded into each other. *We* became *me*. At long last, I was *whole*. My feet found freedom and holding tight to the essence of who I'd become, a woman freed from past horrors, I twirled dervish like, daring a new path.

As I began to fall, a pair of arms encircled me. They were gentle, but oh so firm. What had been dream-like became real.

---

[15] William Woodsworth, 1770-1850, Ode on Intimations of Immortality from Recollections of Early Childhood.

Scene Thirty-Four

As I said, what had been dream-like became real.

David carried me to his campsite, only a short distance up the path. He laid me on his open sleeping bag in his tent. "Undress me," he beseeched while removing my clothes. "Come closer, Fiza, come closer," he begged, pressing me to him. With uncontrolled wildness, we loved each other. Échappé sauté. I was air borne. Every inch of my skin tingled with star light. Together we flew past the moon. Soaring, soaring and somewhere in the celestial mist we exploded. Two butterflies, wafting, and whirling, flitting, and fluttering, danced back to earth. Coming from far off, I heard a human voice, "Fiza, I will love you forever."

And a human voice answered, "This moment, here in a tent in Africa, secure in your arms, is all the forever I ask." Sleep nudged me off to dreamland. As I slipped away, I thought, *dreams will never match the beauty of reality.*

We stayed two days at the camp and made love over and over. Each time we became more controlled, lingering to take in the boundlessness of us, giving and receiving until we could wait no longer to let our worlds unite in ecstasy. We couldn't seem to get enough of each other. It was as if, having waited so long to share this intimacy, we didn't want it to end.

On the first day when we went to fetch water at the creek, David decided that we should investigate. Because the creek water was warm, he had a hunch that something had to be heating it. And sure enough, he was right. We found a natural hot springs pool. The creek formed the overflow. It was heaven to soak in the hot water. We took full advantage, soaking in the mornings when we went to fetch water and again in the evenings to watch the sunsets, before going to bed. My skin became wrinkly clean, and my hair shone.

This time together was precious. We combined our food and camping equipment. One evening when we were about to prepare our meal, David suggested, "If you boil the rice on one of the small propane burners, I'll heat the re-hydrated meal on the other. You have a choice, cheesy chicken with broccoli or lean ground beef with onions, diced tomatoes, and bell peppers."

"I like the spices in the beef dish. The cumin and coriander wafting in the air set the mood." We sat on ground mats and ate, savoring every bite. "I've such an appetite," I exclaimed. "This simple meal tastes better than any banquet at La Grande Maison."

"Have you ever eaten there?" David asked, raising his pinky as if to sip tea in style.

"No, but I can imagine. The water's boiling: shall I make coffee?"

"And I'll warm the dried peaches and pears. Heating them with a sprinkle of water not only makes them softer but it brings out the flavor. Don't you think?"

We made love, we cooked, we soaked and watched the sunset, and, too quickly, the time passed.

Scene Thirty-Five
My Village

S uddenly, my knees weakened. Shaking, I lost control and fell to the ground. Excruciating physical and emotional pain gripped me, and I clenched my stomach, curled in the fetus position, withering. Had the cords that bind, finally, severed? Was I no longer attached to my birth family?

In a few minutes, I recovered and was able to stand and continue. I was going to where I had set up my camp, wanting to have a private, final look where my transformation had taken place. There wasn't a sign that I had even been there. I picked up a small stone and put it in my pocket.

On the third day, we had a quick soak, ate granola for breakfast, and packed up. "David," I said, "I have no need to see my father's place. I'm at peace with where my family is."

"Are you sure, Fiza?" David asked. "You might not come again for some time."

"I'm sure. I see no reason to go to where father's tukul was. It's not that I'm moving on. I'll never forget them. I'm moving forward. But I really need to see if my aunt is still there. That's my purpose. When I'm satisfied, we can leave. We should be able to catch the late plane home."

I was surprised how quickly we got to the village. I had thought it was much farther away. We set our packs under a bush and stood a short distance from my aunt's tukul. Everything was the same, the tukul, the firepit out front, the iroko wood bench and table that sat by the door. The same, but crumbling. Perhaps in my youth, having nothing to compare it with, I didn't notice how grey and dilapidated it was, or more-than-likely, time had taken its toll.

A woman approached us. "Can I be of help?" she asked.

"I'm here to see my aunt," I answered. "I'm Fiza and this is my partner, David."

"Fiza. Oh, Fiza," she squealed, dropping the Gerry cans she was holding. She rushed over and hugged me tight. "I didn't recognize you. I haven't seen you since you left, such a long time ago. We were told that you had gone with that doctor to another country, and now, here you are. By the look on your face, I don't think you recognize me. I'm Nadia."

"Nadia. Nadia. No, I don't recognize you, either. I hugged her, and we kissed on both cheeks.

"Oh, David," she said, putting out her hand, "excuse my manners. I'm pleased to meet you."

"I'm happy to witness such a happy reunion," he said, taking her hand. "Were you going someplace with those Gerry cans? Can I help you?"

"Fiza, I'm sure you're eager to see Mother. Let me tell you, she's fine. I'll go in and tell her that you're here. She'll come out." She turned to David and said, "Let's give them some privacy. You can help me fetch water. We'll need plenty. Mother will have to feed her guests. And we should gather some manioc leaves."

I moved closer to the door. A hunched figure, supported by a walking stick, took a few steps outside. I ran to her and took her in my arms. "Auntie. Auntie," I said in Dinka. "I've come." Fortunately, my dialect wasn't bad, thanks to the ladies at the Juda hospital.

She looked up at me and spoke in a combination of Dinka and English. "I sensed that you were near," she said in English and then in Dinka she added, "I knew you would come."

"Let me help you. Let's sit on the bench," I said, taking her arm. When we were settled, few words passed between us. It wasn't an awkwardness. We were content being together and taking in the precious moment. "I've brought you a gift," I said. "I know it's been a long time coming, but it's my gratitude for everything you did for me." I showed her the gold chain, then reached over and fastened it on her. I placed a roll of currency in her hand and wrapped her fingers around it.

"You are thoughtful, my child," she whispered. Tears caught in the wrinkles in her face. She ignored them, and said, "Your father, my brother, is proud that his eldest daughter hasn't forgotten me. I always said that no news was good news. I kept the faith; and here you are."

My cheeks were also wet, but I tried to be cheerful by saying, "Auntie, can you fill in the years for me? Tell me about your children."

"I have wonderful children. They all make my heart sing. I'm a very proud mother. And I have four grandchildren. I haven't seen them yet, but my sons promise to come home soon and bring them. That will be a happy day."

"Where are your sons?" I asked.

"They are both in the U.S.," she answered. "It's hard for them to come home, but they send letters and Nadia reads them to me."

"How wonderful," I said. "Nadia's speaks English so well. Where was she trained?" I asked.

"Nadia went to England and studied business. She works and lives in town, but comes often to bring me things and check up on me. Nadia wants me to live with her in town, but I was born in this place, and I'll die here." The strength she put into those last words amazed me. I heard echoes of the strong woman of my memories.

David and Nadia returned and prepared the meal in the outdoor firepit. I watched David crush the manioc leaves in a huge stand-up-to mortar and pestle. He caught my eye, and I commented, "You're a natural."

"Oh, I'm no natural, but I'm happy. Does that count for something?"

"It's everything, love," I answered.

Nadia chopped meat and browned it in a heavy iron pot that hung over the fire. "I bring frozen meat from town and hang it down the well to keep," she explained. She stirred in a panful of chopped aubergines, then asked David, "Could you pour water into the pot, please? I'll tell you when." David complied. "Now, we'll put the lid on and let this simmer before we add the manioc leaves and thicken it with okra. Can you help me with the pancakes?"

She patted dough, that looked green because of the finely chopped spring onions, into individual cakes and placed them on a flat iron next to the hanging pot. David's job was to flip them. When the meal was ready, Nadia held a wooden tray with four clay bowls and David dished out the stew. The spicy aroma from the steaming bowls reached me before she set them on the outside table and sat across from me. "Be careful, Mother. It's very hot," she said. David brought the long clay tray, piled high with pancakes, and set it in the middle of the table. He sat across from Auntie.

Before we began, I said, "Thank you, Auntie, for this food. And thank you, Nadia, and David for preparing it."

Nadia said, "Bless this food that we are about to eat."

David touched Auntie's arm. "Thank you," he said, "for welcoming me at your table."

"Let's eat," Auntie answered.

When we had finished eating, Nadia served tea from an enamel pot. "Mother mixes her own tea leaves," she commented. "You mix them according to your mood, do you not, Mother?"

"I'm guided," Auntie said.

"I can smell hibiscus," David said. "Am I right?"

"A sharp nose means a sharp mind. Yes, David, you are right."

A most delicious meal. Given and taken with love. One that I would always remember. I was content, but in the back of my mind, I thought about the plane schedule. Auntie closed her eyes, nodding off. "Come mother," Nadia said, helping Auntie stand. "You need to rest awhile." When she returned, she explained, "It's Mother's way. She sensed that you'd be leaving, and didn't want to say goodbye."

"I'm thankful. I, also, do not want to say goodbye, but the time has come. David, if we leave now, can we catch that late flight?"

"Yes. Nadia, if we leave are camping gear, can you make use of it?"

"Certainly. I'll sell it at the market and give the money to Mother."

He put the things in a neat pile and then said, "I'm glad I came. Fiza talks about her family and this place. It's been nice to experience it for myself. I'll have to get me one of those mortar and pestles."

"I'm happy that I've met you. I'll E-transfer you a mortar and pestle," she added, laughing.

She looked at me, and we walked into a warm hug. "I didn't know what to expect," I said. I didn't know if Auntie was still alive. It's such a relief to see that you are taking good care of her. It should be my duty, also."

"Life has its twists and turns. You came back and that has given her great pleasure. Seeing you well and with a loving partner has been a precious gift for her. If you felt you had a duty, you've paid it a thousand times over. I, too, do not want to say goodbye. Please, Fiza, just walk away."

David and I put on our backpacks and started up the path. At the spot where the path flattened, I did what I didn't do the first time I walked away from my village. I stopped and looked back. The tukuls were hidden by the trees, but I saw smoke rising. It gave me a warm feeling. Perhaps, when I first left, I *had* looked back. *How else did this picture of the smoke rising get stuck in my memory?* That first time, the thought of not returning probably never occurred to me. Now, I know, deep in my being, that I've left my village for good. There will be no road back. I got down on my hands and knees, took the small stone from my pocket and buried it. I kissed my birth earth. This ritual was my way of saying goodbye to my past. The first time I left, I didn't cry. Now, the parched earth drank my tears. With determined resolve, I stood and said, "Let's go."

Part Three
Return to Örnsköldsvik, Sweden

Scene Thirty-Six

Going Home

D avid set a fast pace. I couldn't talk and keep up with him. He noticed I was having difficulties and started talking to slow down. "When we were picking manioc leaves, Nadia warned me about their poisonous stems. Teasing her, I picked up a stem and pretended to take a bite, 'Shall I test your theory?' I asked.

'Ooof,' she said, raising an eyebrow. 'Take heed. You don't want to do that.'

'My, oh my,' I said, 'you are so much like Fiza.'

'Why wouldn't I be? What's the saying? We are two apples on different branches of our family tree,' she retorted.

'That's not exactly how the saying goes, but I like it,' I said.

"Fiza let's stop and have a drink. We don't want to become dehydrated. Nadia boiled the water, so not to worry."

I stopped, sat down on the path, and sipped some water from the canteen. "Isn't it interesting that no matter how we jumble a saying, people usually understand?" I said.

"Isn't it the truth?" he answered.

We rested a few minutes, then I got to my feet, and we carried on. In no time we were at Juda town.

"This was so much shorter than when I was going the other way," I exclaimed.

"Distance and time are illusions. They both depend on the circumstances. When you were going down, you didn't know what you might face, and you weren't in any hurry to find out. I know because I was following your painfully slow pace."

We found a taxi, and David paid the driver handsomely to take us quickly to the airport. He sped, dodging the potholes with finesse, and we arrived at the airport with an hour to spare. Because he had left-over local currency, David tipped the smiling driver. For this one trip, he probably had a week's wages in his pocket. He drove away with his head held high.

"I'm going to the ladies' room to freshen up," I said.

"Fine. I'll try my luck at texting Mr. Doc," he answered. He pulled his phone with the attached charger from a pocket of his cargo pants. "I want to give him our flight numbers and when we are expected to be in Ornskoldsvik."

"That's great."

In the ladies' room, I was delighted by the tap water. *What a novelty.* I smiled. I splashed my face with cold water, brushed my teeth, and ran my wet fingers through my hair. I shook out navy travelling pants and a sweater. Because no one was around, I undressed and put on fresh outerwear. When I was dressed, I glanced in the mirror that had seen better days. *You look gorgeously presentable*, I told myself, trying to boost my morale.

When I came out, I saw David, in dark slacks and a matching, long-sleeved Henley, leaning against a pillar. As I approached, he said, "You look lovely, my dear."

"And you look dapper," I answered.

"It wasn't anything like our hot springs, but I washed and brushed my teeth," he said.

"Did you have any luck with texting?"

"It took three tries. I was about to give up when the digital gods whisked my message away."

We checked our backpacks through to Ornskoldsvik, each keeping a small carry-on bag. We had no problems getting through customs. When we were boarded and settled in our seats, David asked, "How do you feel?"

I looked at the date on my boarding pass. May fourteen. I had been away seven and a half months. It felt like an eternity. "I don't know, David," I answered. "I really don't know. So much has happened over such a short time. I feel emotionally exhausted. I wonder if I'll ever set both of my feet in one time zone."

"What do you mean?" he asked.

"I'll live in Sweden, but there will always be a longing for my birthland. When I die, please scatter my ashes in both places." He squeezed my hand. I took that to mean he may not understand but he had heard me.

"When the plane reaches its highest altitude, the steward will pass out warm cloths," he said. "Then, you must close your eyes and cover them with the cloth. You should try to nap. I'll wake you when the food cart comes."

"Thank you, David. But what about you?"

"I'm fine. Don't forget, I've been through the trenches," he said. "I'll nap after eating."

After our stopover in Germany, we were rested. "Let's make wedding plans," David suggested.

What a wonderful way to pass the time on a flight. We arranged everything, at least on paper, right down to the color of the napkins on the reception table. Time flew by and before we knew it, we had landed at Ornskoldsvik. As we pushed our carts up the arrival ramp, I spotted Mom and Dad. I left my cart and ran to them. We fell into a three-person hug. "Welcome home, Fiza," Dad said, kissing me. "I now must go and rescue, David. You've stranded him with the luggage."

"Oh, Fiza," Mom whispered into my hair. "I was so worried. I'm happy you're back safely."

"I'm happy to be home," was all I could blubber while wiping at my tears. We linked arms and walked towards Dad and David. They were hugging each other, patting each other's backs.

"Mission accomplished," David said.

"I didn't doubt you for a moment," Dad said. "Thank you."

David hugged Mom, and she kissed him on the cheek. "You've kept your word. I'm thankful, a million times over," she said. "Look, we're blocking traffic. Let's get to the car. We can talk on the way in."

David offered to drive, but Dad thanked him and said, "Not after all that flying. You'll be too wobbly. You can be my co-pilot."

Mom and I sat at the back. When we were on our way, I took her hand and said, "Mom I have something to tell you."

"And what's that?" she asked.

"On the plane, David and I made wedding plans."

"How wonderful. Have you set a date?"

David looked backed. "Yes," he said. "Two weeks from now, on Saturday."

"Oh my," Mom gasped. "Two weeks? Sister Ellie's living back at home. She's finished her internship at the hospital and has moved out of residence. She'll be a great help. But the boys, I hope they can get home with such short notice. Tomorrow, after you've rested, you must come to dinner. We'll hear your plans and get started right away. There's a lot of work to be done."

"Mrs. Doc," David said. "Please don't get stressed. It's going to be very casual. We want it to be a happy affair. Fiza and I will do most of the work. When you hear our plans, you'll see, there's no need for anyone to be stressed."

"For a moment, Fiza, when you said you had something to tell me, I thought you were going to say you were pregnant. I wondered how I would feel about that, but it's a wedding. I guess I can put those other feelings on the back burner, for now, and just enjoy this celebration," Mom said.

"We haven't got to planning about babies, yet. But you'll be the first to know. You can bet on that," I said.

David had parked his car at my parent's place. We transferred our stuff, thanked Mom and Dad, and headed to the turret. Jet lag was setting in, and we barely exchanged a word. I put my hand on his shoulder, and every now and then, we smiled at each other. We left our luggage in the trunk of the car and climbed the stairs with just our carry-ons. "How good to be home," I said. "Let's shower and go to bed."

Scene Thirty-Seven

Gertrude's Hour

I woke late. David wasn't in bed, but he had clipped a note to his pillow. *My sleeping beauty, I must run and do a few errands. I'll be back soon. Please don't go to The Store without me. I want to be with you when you see Gertrude. xoxox D.*

I walked around the turret, touching my books, handling the glass pieces, checking the potted black pansies. The note I had left David in the pansy pot was gone. *He never mentioned it. Would it have disintegrated in the months I had been away*? "I missed you, my home sweet home," I said. After a long shower, I put on a light pantsuit and waited for David. Soon, I heard him bounding up the stairs. He burst in, excited, "My, you look pretty in pink," he said, hugging me. "You must come, I've made breakfast for you in The Store kitchen."

"Sounds good," I said, kissing his cheek. "I'm starving."

The path to The Store was delightful. The scent of pine mixed with the blooming of lavender was so much not Africa. Bees buzzed and birds chirped.

We walked into a roar of "Surprise" and "Welcome Back." My hands flew to my mouth, and I gasped. Rose and blue balloons filled the room and were taped to the ceiling. A table decorated with blue heather was laden with finger foods. A tower of cold shrimp and a platter stacked with different colored cheeses caught my eye. Sue popped open a bottle from an ice bucket.

"Everyone has been working all morning," David said. "Huong stood guard. If you came, she was prepared to wrestle you to the ground to keep you from spoiling their surprise."

"Thank you. Thank you, all. It's a wonderful surprise, and I'm happy to be home. I'm starving. Shall we eat?"

"Wait, wait, I, too, have a surprise," David announced, holding up his arms and walking towards Gertrude. Sue passed around glasses of the bubbly. David pulled multiple levers. Gertrude grunted. The women were so silent it was if they were holding their breaths. Gertrude clinked-clanked, as if in protest. She shook, and then gave up. *Oh, no.* David pushed the levers back in place. Then he pulled them once more. Gertrude grunted even more fiercely. She shuttered. *Please, Grampa Y.* Gertrude clinked-clanked, clinked-clanked, shook herself out, and her parts began to move.

I looked at David. Beads of perspiration gathered on his brow. After a minute, he shouted, "She's weaving." We clapped and cheered. Some jumped up and popped balloons, adding to the uproar.

I ran to David and hugged him tightly. "Thank you, love. Thank you. You came to Africa and gave me a surprise of a lifetime. Now this. It has me flying off the highest mountain. Thank you."

"You're welcome, my love. I thank you for giving me a second chance." We kissed.

Everyone raised their glasses and I said, "Skal, Gertrude. Well done." Gertrude, honored, clinked-clanked away in earnest, leaving us to party.

I saw the different shades of David as he transformed over the past year and a half. David grinning, leaning against my door frame the day I met him. The supportive David, seeing me through my own transformations. The sincere David, that I've come to love so very deeply. The David I want to spend the rest of my life with. I couldn't hold back the tears. They spilled out like a dam burst, and the river ran down my face in torrents. David wiped my face with a napkin. I raised my glass to the girls and said, "It's my party. I'll cry if I want to."

They raised theirs, "Cheers, Fiza."

Sue near shouted, "Here's to the best damn boss on the planet."

"And the loveliest," David added.

Gertrude ignored us and went on her merry way, clink-clanking.

I bundled up my happiness and put it in a room in my memory. I left the door open.

Scene Thirty-Eight

The Wedding

I was glad that I'd chosen not to have a bridal bouquet. The carpet laid over the sand between the rows of chairs wasn't exactly solid. I needed to hang on to Dad's arm with both hands to steady myself. Besides, sister Ellie had entwined black pansies and white forget-me-nots into a lovely tiara and pinned it in my hair. I thought it was more *me,* and it would work as well as a bouquet to throw to the single females at the reception. As the family gathered, I said to Gramma Tree and Mom, "I've folded Gertrude's first two blankets on your chairs. They are yours."

"After the wedding, I'll package my blanket and send it to my sister, Ellie Mae," Gramma Tree said. "After all, she was the one that found Gertrude. It's a shame she wasn't up to the flight and must miss this day."

"How thoughtful," I said, giving her a hug. "Gertrude will make you another. She's a busy gal. Gramma Tree, Paul will escort you to your seat in the front row, and Mom, Chriz will escort you. The boys will stand guard on either side of the arch decorated with red camellia. It's as splendid as the two of you. Do you like your corsage, Gramma Tree?"

"I love it, dear. It's so fragrant. I did just fine pinning on your mom's, but, in her nervousness, she pricked me twice. I see the boutonnieres also have a camellia. With his allergies, Chriz had better keep his nose up wind."

"A work friend of David's is playing David's guitar. He'll hold it close to the mic, but with this wind, the people down the beach may hear it, and we may not. Music or not, Paul will keep you in step, Gramma Tree, but Mom, you and Chriz, having two left feet will have to do the best you can." We laughed. They knew I was trying to calm myself, as well as them.

I had a few moments, and I thought about what David had told me about Paul and Chriz. He told me that they were a great help setting up the sound system and the outdoor heaters. He said, "You should have seen Paul trying to hold down the canopy while Chriz and I struggled to fasten it to the ground. The wind was gusting, and I feared that the canopy, with Paul dangling, might go flying out to sea. We had fun." It made me happy that David was getting to know my brothers.

Before Gramma Tree and Mom started out, I reminded them, "The Justice of the Peace should also be in the front row. He's here to bear witness. He'll be the one trying to keep the marriage certificate from blowing away."

"I know him. Beats me that he's old enough for such a responsible job. I'll keep a sharp eye on him," Gramma Tree said, winking.

When the others had gone down the aisle, and Dad and I waited for our cue, Dad looked at me and said, "Fiza, sweetheart. This is the longest walk you'll take in your life."

"How so? Dad."

"You're walking from singledom to marrydom. Don't expect that there won't be any pitfalls."

I squeezed his arm tight and said, "Ooof." He understood that to mean everything—thank you, I love you, and just because I'm going to that new land doesn't mean I'll forget you and Mom and everything that you both have given me.

The guitar blasted forth with the classical Wedding March. Dad and I started. I smiled at the guests. It pleased me to see many of the partners of the girls from The Store. I seldom get to see them. In appreciation of everyone's coming, Dad gave out nods. Halfway down the aisle, a mighty gust of wind flapped the long full skirt of my golden-rod-yellow dress, threatening to raise it to embarrassing heights. Fortunately, I had the free hand to make it behave. I was thankful to have chosen long sleeves— narrow down the arm and puffed at the shoulder. Huong, from The Store, had painstakingly decorated the sleeves and the waist with seed pearls. I felt like a princess.

David stood on the other side of the arch. When we reached it, Dad took my hand and gave it to David. I stepped through. Dad waited until we were settled at the front, then he skirted the arch and took his place next to David. Chriz was sneezing up a storm. Dad signaled to him, and he went and stood next to our father. Dad removed Chriz's boutonniere and pinned it on his lower pocket.

Ellie, in a sky blue, three-quarters length satin dress that wasn't behaving any better than mine, walked towards us. Her small bouquet of trailing ivy, white forget-me-nots, and red camellias, swayed. Paul stepped with her through the arch and planted her by my side. He stood next to her. Later, Paul told me, "Ellie was fluttering like a butterfly. You can't imagine how difficult it was to keep her from flying off," he said.

All my men, so handsome in royal blue tuxedoes and bow ties. Apparently, when it came to color choice, Dad, adamantly, was not for black. "This is a beginning; not an ending," he declared. The others, understanding his meaning, agreed on blue. Whenever they moved, their golden-rod-yellow cummerbunds flashed.

Chriz's sneezing appeared to abate, so David and I looked at each other. I took his left hand and said, "David, with this ring, I promise to be faithful to you. I'll do my best to make our partnership fulfilling and happy. I swear that I'm sincere. I do." I slipped the ring on his finger.

David took my left hand and looked into my eyes. To my great surprise, he sang his version of Hank Snow's, "With this Ring."

"With this ring I Thee wed an angel here beside me,

A moment more and heaven will be mine,

With this ring I Thee wed, I vow I love you truly,

And every day you'll hear me say, "I do."

He slipped the ring on my finger. We flew into each other's arms and sealed our vows with a deep, warm marriage kiss. The guests went wild, standing, clapping, whistling, chanting, "Fiza and David. Fiza and David."

The Justice of the Peace brought the marriage certificate for us to sign. The guests chanted us through the signing. When we stood, Dad hushed them to make an announcement. "I ask you to join in the car parade as we go to the Karaoke Café," he said. "We wish to refresh and feed you. And there'll be music and dancing. Please come and enjoy yourselves. The wedding car will lead the way."

When we entered the café, it was unrecognizable. It was filled with black and white streamers and balloons that swung from the ceiling. My breath caught. "Oh, the beauty of it," I gasped. "How royal-looking."

"Perfect for Prince charming and his princess," Naslund, who stood with Prince by the side of the entrance, commented. He looked so sharp in a suit that he, also, was barely recognizable. Prince's studded collar sparkled under the twinkling lights that draped around the room.

"Good dog," David said, giving Prince a treat from his pocket.

"Thank you, Naslund and Prince," I said, and stepped into the room. Black and white striped cloths dressed the tables that circled the dance floor. Pure white dinnerware. Shining silver that the café used only on special occasions. Each table was centered with a twelve-inch puffed-up, simulated black pansy. They were so delicately authentic, I thought I caught a whiff of their gentle spicy fragrance. Huong designed them, and all the girls at The Store helped to get them made on time.

People, long after the wedding, would bring up the topic and tell me how scrumptious the meal was. At the table, I recall Paul declaring, "This is the best Cornish hen I've ever tasted."

"The stuffing is almost as good as yours, Mom," Chriz added.

"Who would think of finely chopping green and red peppers and stirring them into the mashed potatoes?" Mom asked. "I like the color and the crunch."

"I've never had white asparagus," Gramma Tree exclaimed. "And whatever it is that they've drizzled is so tasty."

"It's balsamic vinegar," David said. "White asparagus with balsamic vinegar, straight from Modena, Italy, is the house special."

"Yummy," Ellie agreed. A waiter, pushing a trolley of drinks, asked if he could top ours up. "Yes, please," Ellie said. "I would like sparkling rosé, if I may."

"Ruinart Rosé, for the lady," the waiter said, handing her a fresh bubbling glass.

Dad raised his glass and looking at Mom said, "You've done a wonderful job choosing the menu, Tijay. The noise level has declined considerably. People must be enjoying their meal. Thank you."

"Skal." Everyone agreed.

I'll never forget the wedding cake—all five tiers of it wobbling as Mom wheeled the cart into the center of the room. I like the old tradition of the bride and groom feeding the cake to each other. The original meaning of this act is probably lost in history, but David and I had fun with it, and ended up getting more on our faces than in our mouths. The rest of the cake was cut and served as dessert, along with coffee or tea.

Then came the Wedding Dance. This dance was nothing like our first dance, almost exactly a year ago. Today's my wedding day, I kept telling myself. A date to remember the rest of my life. The first day of June. On our first date, jiving, David flung me away from him and then twirled me close. Now, he held me close, as if he would never let me go. As we clung, Louis Armstrong sang, "It's a Wonderful World." Singing into my hair, David joined him for the last three lines:

> "And I think to myself what a wonderful world.
> Yes, I think to myself what a wonderful world.
> Yes, I think to myself what a wonderful world."

The guests banged their silverware against their glasses as a signal for us to kiss. We kissed. That kiss told me that David and I, in our wonderful new world, had found love, everlasting.

Author's Notes:

Black Pansies is not a book of hummingbirds and honeysuckle, even though in her sometimes-mystical words, which often reflect nature, we hear the gentleness of Fiza's heritage and a surprising kindness, unexpected because it comes from someone who was terribly abused as a child.

The story is about love and loss, longing and belonging, the dynamics of identity, and the complexities of the human condition.

Fiza offers us an intimate glimpse into who she and David are, their inner struggles, their dogged-determination to become whole, to have the life of their dreams—a mate, a family, everlasting love.

I rejoice because Fiza is finally able to think: **"The world as it is is enough."**—*Cloud Cuckoo Land* by Anthony Doer.

"We're all different. We're all misfits. And nothing gives us better wings in life than understanding how we fit in the world."

—Andreas Souvaliotis.

Acknowledgements

Books that influenced the writing of Black Pansies

Behrouz Boochani, No Friend but the Mountains.
Carlos Castaneda, The Teachings of Don Juan.
Marlene F Cheng, Temptation and Surrender.
—, The Fallen Sniper Tears.
—, A Mystical Embrace.
—, The Madam's Friend.
Alephonsion Deng, Benson Deng and Benjamin Ajok with Judy A. Berstein, They Poured Fire on Us from the Sky.
Joan Didion, The Year of Magical Thinking.
Anthony Doerr, Cloud Cuckoo Land.
Dr. Wayne W. Dyer, Inspiration.
Omar el Akkad, What Strange Paradise.
Tan Twan Eng, The Garden of Evening Mists.
Kahlil Gibran, The Prophet.
Michelle Good, Five Little Indians.
Emaculee Ilibagiza, Left to Tell.
Hilda F. Johnson, South Sudan: The Untold Story.
Dalai Lama and Victor Chan, Wisdom of Forgiveness.
John O'Donohue, Beauty.
—, Eternal Echoes.
—, Anam Cara.
Boris Pasternak, Doctor Zhivago.
Ben Rawlence, The City of Thorns.
Lisa See, Snow Flower and the Secret Fan.
Nick Turse, Next Time They'll Come to Count the Dead: War and Survival in South Sudan.
Shell Zanne, Only the Beginning.

Thank you to all my beta readers and reviewers. A very special thanks to Kirsten McNeill at Worthy Writers Editing. Your meticulous editing lifted the book far beyond my imaginings. Your bent for perfection blew me away, and I am most grateful.

I am indebted to Pamela Magee, owner of The Macgee Cloth Company in Roberts Creek on the beautiful sunshine Coast of B.C., Canada. Her company specializes in blankets and throws made on an antique English shuttle loom. All my information on antique looms came from Pamela. Thank you, so much, Pamela. When Covid settles, I'll take the ferry, visit your studio, and watch the loom doing its amazing weaving.

Many thanks to "I want to be your computer guy."–Danny Cheng at ideaworks@shaw.ca. Without your technical help, it couldn't have been done.

About The Author

Marlene was prairie-born, farm-raised, and now lives among the old-growth pine and cedar, overlooking the Pacific Ocean on the West Coast of Canada.

She is a Maincrest Media and Book Excellence awards-winning author of women's fiction.

Her books are about the relationships that define women's lives—romance, friendship, family.

Marlene is a keen observer of how people think and feel, and she writes lyrical, uplifting, and emotionally rich stories.

She is a coauthor of *Love Wins, A Ukraine Charity Anthology*, which reached the Top 100 in Amazon's Best Seller's Rank.

Marlene's Other Books

The Many Layered Skirt
Shifting to Freedom
Temptation and Surrender
The Fallen Sniper Tears
A Mystical Embrace
The Madam's Friend
The Inspector's Daughter and The Maid

As an author I highly appreciate the feedback I get from readers. If you enjoyed this book, please consider leaving a short review or a few positive words on any of the following sites:
amazon.com/author/marlenecheng
goodreads.com/marlenecheng
marlenecheng.com
I look forward to hearing from you at marlene.cheng@telus.net. I read all reviews and respond.
THANK YOU

The Inspector's Daughter and The Maid is a moving and delightful blend of **historical** and **speculative romance fiction.**

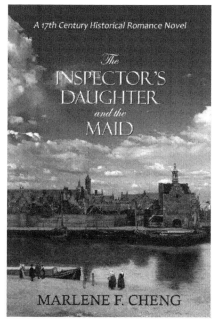

The foundations of traditional structures reveal themselves to be no longer stone, but sand, and in the hearts of **the Inspector's Daughter and the Maid** some natural ease gets broken, and their trust in **a promising future loses its innocence.**

In **the severance of winds**, beyond their wildest dreams, **possibilities are awakened**.

Which one will win the heart of the wealthy merchant's son - the Music Teacher?

What Beta Readers said about The Inspector's Daughter and the Maid.

"The author takes us to another time and place with authenticity and a strong feminist story."

—Diana Jewel, M.A., Mission, Canada

"Amidst current travel restrictions, this novel is a special treat. The author took me on a journey through time and place to 17th century Delft. With tremendous heart and a fluid writing style, Marlene Cheng wove a tale which captivated me from the very first page, putting me in the shoes of her protagonists and fully engaging me in their trials until the very end."

—Desiree Sy, Milan, Italy.

"The Inspector's Daughter had me gripped from the very beginning. Marlene successfully throws the reader into the past and into the characters' lives. You live through the characters' lives right along side them and are rooting for them every step of the way. I couldn't recommend this book more, I can't wait to see what the author does next!"

—Clare Appezzato, editorial, WordWorks magazine, Federation of BC writers.

Check out The Inspector's Daughter and the Maid on my website: marlenecheng.com.

Manufactured by Amazon.ca
Bolton, ON

30919398R00114